PICTURE OF DEATH

I pointed the camera down and squeezed the release to check its operation. At the same moment, I heard the thin, almost inaudible passage of the masher beam from a sniper's weapon, and my body, remembering its combat-learned lessons, dropped me flat. Yet even as I went down I saw, following the pointing of my camera, a snaking, living gash forming itself in the garish pattern of the floor of the magician's platform.

In a flash of understanding as brilliant as only hindsight can be, I realized that someone had replaced my photographic laser with a high-intensity killer unit—and I couldn't shut it off!

I fought to keep the camera from slipping out of my grip. Fought to hold on to it and keep it pointed away from the now roiling, screaming mass of children around me.

Fighting the laser beam, and swearing at the animals who, to kill a man, would choose a time and a weapon that, like a hose that could not be turned off, would spray its death at the youngsters pressing close around him. . . .

DAW Books Presents Frank A. Javor's
Rim-World™ Novels:

THE RIM-WORLD™ LEGACY *And Beyond*

SCOR-STING

THE ICE BEAST

THE RIM-WORLD™ LEGACY
AND BEYOND

FRANK A. JAVOR

DAW BOOKS, INC.
DONALD A. WOLLHEIM, FOUNDER
375 Hudson Street, New York, NY 10014
ELIZABETH R. WOLLHEIM
SHEILA E. GILBERT
PUBLISHERS

THE RIM-WORLD™ LEGACY *And Beyond*, copyright © 1991 by Frank A. Javor.

The Rim-World™ Legacy, copyright © 1967 by Frank A. Javor; copyright renewed by the author.

Heavy, Heavy, copyright © 1963 by Frank A. Javor, copyright renewed by the author; this story originally appeared in *Amazing Stories*.

Moire, copyright © 1991 by Frank A. Javor.

Rim-World℠ is a trademark of Frank A. Javor.

All Rights Reserved.

Cover art by Nicholas Jainschigg.

DAW Book Collectors No. 860.

First Printing, September 1991

1 2 3 4 5 6 7 8 9

DAW TRADEMARK REGISTERED
U.S. PAT. OFF. AND FOREIGN COUNTRIES
—MARCA REGISTRADA.
HECHO EN U.S.A.

PRINTED IN THE U.S.A.

Contents

THE RIM-WORLD™ LEGACY   7

HEAVY, HEAVY   209

MOIRE   230

AUTHOR'S NOTE

"Moire" was to have been Pike's second short adventure on Poldrogi. It metamorphosed, instead, into THE RIM-WORLD™ LEGACY and his first appearance in a novel. His first encounter with print was in the short story "Heavy, Heavy."

Prologue

I'm six-four, weigh two hundred Earth pounds, and swim about as well as the proverbial rock. All the same, I pressed myself down into the shallow black water from which the sparse weeds sprang, listening.

Listening. Straining my ears in the heavy darkness until I thought the skin on the back of my neck would pop, knowing all the while that the rise and fall of the sounds that I heard those who were after me making was not caused by their nearness or distance, but by me.

Warily, silently swearing at the way the strength in my hands came and went, I began working away at the base of a tall reed. Bending it. Pulling it down to me slowly, all the time aware to the point of torture that in the night-vision glasses the men hot on my trail were sure to be wearing, a movement, unless it was heartbreakingly slow, would show as a sudden flaring of bright yellow against the dull red of the overall background stillness.

"Pike," someone shouted, his voice coming at a low point in my hearing, but I could still make out my own name well enough.

"Pike. Come out. Give yourself up. Don't make us come in after you."

Give myself up? There were children's and women's voices mingling with those of the men hunting me, and the sound of them added that thin frosting of urgency to my predicament that had me fighting to hold at bay the unreasoning temptation to break and run. Break and run and evade my pursuers by sheer animal speed.

Sheer animal speed against the animal thing after me. The thing that brought with it to the hunt its women and children. The thing that by this act betrayed itself to me to be no policeman's posse that might be content to capture and to hold me.

The thing that cried out to me to give myself up to it, the thing that was a howling mob.

I felt panic trying to force its treacherous way into the racing of my mind.

I fought against it and kept inching the reed down slowly, fearful that it would slip from my weakening grasp and the motion of its snapping erect would betray my location as surely as if I'd sent up a flare.

Fighting, for the same reason, the urge to shake my head to ease the prickling of the old scar I could feel throbbing on the top of my balding head. The scar that was a souvenir of the Second Police Action. Thin, all but invisible, it seemed to have a sensor of its own that made it tingle when it thought I was about to head into something that, if I was lucky, I'd live to regret.

The reed. At last I had it flat in the water and hidden from surface view, close to my body.

I began twisting it. *Slowly, slowly, but hurry, before they can rig and bring up the heat detectors that will make of the warmth of your body a beacon to home in on.*

Twisting the reed. Silently berating my hands for their unsure grip that was making of so simple a task so formidable a project. Fighting to keep my lungs from gasping out air and making the high grasses around me tremble. Make them tremble and let the motion betray me to my pursuers.

I felt the reed weakening and then it was free in my grasp.

I strangled my gasp of relief and, forcing myself to wait until I felt my hold firming, I broke off the tip. Then, raising one end to my mouth, gagging momentarily at the brackish taste, I blew into it.

I blew, or tried to; feeling my cheeks puff out and straining until the pinpoints of light danced red and yellow in my eyeballs and the strength of my lungs ebbed away.

Nothing.

The reed was plugged. *Membranes, solid, crossing its diameter.*

Pressed down in the chill water but sweating, I groped in the darkness for another reed. Thin but sturdy.

I found one, pulled it down and worked it free as carefully I had the first even though now I could sense, dimly, and more clearly, and then dimly again as my hearing phased in and out, the unmistakable beat of hover-craft approaching.

Hover-craft that would have heat-detecting units jury-rigged on long cables to hang below and sweep close to the water in their search for the warmth of my body. My head, my face would be enough.

Hover-craft, more than one from the sound, and sooner than I'd expected. They could only be units commandeered from the spaceport that was the chief reason for Poldrogi's existence. The planet's city police could not have been cleared to move outside their jurisdiction so quickly. The men in those hover-craft would be as free of official control as the mob on the ground.

Hurry now, hurry, but do not move with anything but agonizing slowness lest your motion flare brightly yellow in the night-vision glasses of your hunters.

Using the thinner reed as a reamer, I poked into the larger one, first from one end and then from the other.

Again I blew into it and this time I felt my breath unobstructed. The inner passage of the long reed was clear.

Trailing my new-made tube, and stopping only when the drag of the water threatened to wrest it from my fingers when their strength temporarily waned, I moved out in the darkness, feeling blindly for deeper water. Oddly enough, though not even the SpaceNav experts back in my service days had been able to teach me to swim, I had no particular fear of deep water. And if I'd had, the clatter of the hover-craft, now clearly heard in the night behind me, would have given me reason enough to press on.

From the sound of things, it was plain to me that I'd just about had all the time I was going to get to find out how deep the semi-swamps that were the so-called lakes of Poldrogi could get to be.

I found a clump of weeds that felt a little thicker to my groping fingers than the rest and, blowing through my reed to clear it, put one end among them in the hope that it might better escape the notice of my pursuers.

The other end of my reed I took into my mouth and, pinching my nose between my fingers as best their phasing strength would permit me, I let myself settle down, the black water closing over my head, plugging my ears with its characteristic roar, until I sat on the silted and treacherous-feeling bottom.

I hoped that once I was lost to their night-vision glasses they would not continue to search for me until there was daylight enough to see me by.

I was lucky, I suppose, that this was Poldrogi and not Linedo or Paxor or any one of the more fashionable tourist planets that made their scenery a feature, flooding it with lights that came on automatically at the approach of a human.

Poldrogi was, after all, no more than a transit world. A place to transship cargoes or wait out starship connections and, aside from the anticrime lights in the spaceport city itself, its Council of Peers was not going to waste power on lighting up the countryside.

All I could do for now was wait, knowing that the hover-craft, their heat detectors dangling beneath them, were crisscrossing over my head.

Wait in the pulsing water and hope that my breath, traveling the length of the reed I'd selected, would emerge in a wisp cool enough to escape discovery.

A search robot, unlike a hover-craft, I knew would not be commandeered and sent in after me. They were designed to keep the starships and their cargo holds clear of stowaways and other unwanted visitors and would not function in deep water. But someone might think of searching the bills of lading of the docked and docking ships in the hope of finding in one of the transiting shipments an android hunter on its way to a sporting world. And

I could not hide from myself the knowledge that if it were activated and sent to ferret me out, I would stand no chance against a thing that only *looked* like a man.

I pushed the unsettling thought to the back of my mind. To give it play now, when I was over my head in black water, trying to ignore the unseen things that bumped and slithered against me, would only help build the kind of panic that would destroy me.

No. For now the only thing you can do is wait. Wait and try to think of how you got into this predicament in the first place. Then, maybe you will be better able to figure out what to do when you get out and away from here. If you get out and away from here. If....

Stop. Stop thinking if. Stop thinking if anything. Think of the girl.

The girl. The woman. She had been standing by the open transhaus window looking out when I stepped in through the corridor door.

Chapter One

Poldrogi.

I came awake to the sound of a pounding on the panel at the side of my head and the sight of a sterile blue-green surface so close to my face as to seem to be pressing down upon me.

Bunk. I'm in my bunk, but I feel heavy; planet heavy. Why should I feel so heavy? The grav units ... something wrong with the ship's grav units. Trouble ... the pounding in my ear....

Then it came to me where I was. I shook my head and blinked, trying to clear my sleep-clogged eyes and throat and nose of the acrid chemical bite of the disinfected air washing over me.

There were no grav units for something to be wrong with. The pull on my body was a natural one. I was not back in my bunk aboard the *SpyEye IV*, but in a Poldrogi transhaus sleep cubicle, and the pounding I was hearing was someone in the corridor outside banging on the narrow door of my coffinlike enclosure.

I slid back the flimsy plastic panel. "What do you want?" I said. "My time's not up." I fumbled in the wall pocket behind my head for my wrist-chrono. "I've got two ... maybe three hours...."

The fat man standing in the corridor showed me his handmade Poldrogi teeth. "Lady to see you," he said, giving the first word the local accent that made it sound like "lead-y."

"Upstairs. My office," he said full into my face.

Lord, do they even make their transhaus managers eat those miserable disinfectants?

I stared at his fat face peering in at me. Who knew I was here? Who even knew I was alive?

Lady, he'd called her, and I knew trans-world locals well enough to know that if that's what he called her, then that was what she was, and not some corridor-walker trying to drum up a little trade with an ex-SpaceNav Photo Mate.

And with starship passage rates being figured not by the person, but by the pound, anyone with *his* heft couldn't afford to be anything but a local. Space warp technique or no, it still took power and money to move a weight from one place to another. It would take plenty of both to move him.

"A lady?" I said. "For me? Are you sure?"

"She ask for photographer. You it."

Photographer. Then she'd asked for me, not by name, but by occupation. It could mean she had a job she wanted done. It could also mean she wasn't too sure how simon-pure an assignment it was. A lady with a clean photo job in mind doesn't go down into a spaceport transhaus to find someone to do it for her.

My guess was that she wasn't too sure about that part of it, and she was looking for a photographer who needed the money.

I was a photographer ... and I needed the money. Lord, did I need the money. I could at least listen to what she had in mind.

I pushed the panel all the way back and slid out of my cubicle. "Thanks," I said to the fat manager. "Thank you for calling me."

He showed me his hand-carved teeth again. "Nothing to thank for. You only such one here. I tell lady you come."

I watched him shuffle away from me. He was broad, but then the corridor wasn't any wider than it needed to be and he just about filled it with his beam. The scuffs, the crushed shorts, the T-shirt he had on may once have had vibrant color to them, but the constant washing, the sterilizing that transhaus regulations called for had long ago bleached it out until now they looked to have been dipped in drying and faded blood.

It was clean, all right. It was cheap, but it wasn't fancy.

I snaked my travel jumpsuit out of the mesh bag at the back of the cubicle, gave it a token shake to free it of the wrinkles it had picked up, stepped into it. The zipper was stiff, its tab skimpy, but I managed to work it closed and stood for a moment wondering if it would look better if I took my cameras with me or left them until I'd heard what the woman upstairs wanted of me.

I snorted. Why be cute and pretend that my tongue wasn't hanging out for the job? If she hadn't thought whoever she found here would be eager, she wouldn't have come to this place.

I glanced down at my low, tropic-weight boots. They were badly travel-scuffed, but did it matter?

I pressed my thumb against the lockplate of the safebox at the foot of the bunk-shaped cubicle, waited for the "ding" that would show that the print had been recognized and, when it came, raised up the narrow lid and lifted out my cameras.

My record unit. Smaller than a deck of cards, it stored its images on a coil of split-8 metallic foil and could shoot them individually or in a continuous strip that ran for eleven minutes at a speed of one exposure every half second.

For light, it had twin electronic flashtubes, one behind each of the tiny windows at the upper corners. These could be fired individually or together, or adjusted to go off alternately when the camera was set for continuous operation.

Shockproof, watertight, I used it for the things I needed to keep a record of or didn't want the bother of copying. Client agreements, setups I might need to repeat, ship schedules. It went into the small zippered pocket on the left sleeve of my jumpsuit.

And my pretty camera. Correspondent type, but larger than most carried, I'd had it specially fitted with a pic-hold finder that let me see what I'd caught before I permanentized the matching hologram record.

It had cost me all of my severance pay and a little more, but at the time I figured it was worth it. A man is no better than the tools of his trade, that sort of thinking. I also had high hopes of opening up the star worlds with it.

Only the star worlds didn't much seem to care if a balding, ex-SpaceNav Photo Mate opened them up or not. Everything within reasonable reach of my cameras had already been more than thoroughly opened up or was being eyed by a major network so that, in my hunt for something fresh enough to jolt someone into an acceptance, I found myself drifting more and more off the beaten spaceways that marked the population flow in toward the center of the galaxy, and farther and farther out along the loose spiral of its arms to where its rim trailed off into the intergalactic void.

That I should be the only photographer loose in a transit world gasthaus did not particularly surprise me. Poldrogi's topside hostels were not particularly overlarded with swank, but they did have infinitely more appeal for men with firm contracts and expense accounts. Or even with paying contracts alone.

Automatically, and from long habit, before I slung my camera by its strap around my neck I checked the charge of my recording chamber and of the short-pulse, low-intensity laser speedlight and its synchronized reference-beam emitter that nestled close up under the flaring and filter-shielded hologram aperture.

I checked my sleep cubicle a final time to make sure I hadn't forgotten anything, gave the scar on my head a thorough rubbing that I hoped would last it for a while, and walked to the end of the narrow corridor.

I walked past the other cubicle panels, open and shut. It was more like walking through a mausoleum than a hostelry for the living. I came to the end of the corridor and started up the spiraling ramp that led to the surface level and the fat manager's office.

Chapter Two

The manager had his door slid back against Poldrogi's airless heat and I saw her standing at the open window opposite before I rapped on the scrubbed-white jamb.

She turned at the sound, moving with a suppleness that made my eyes instinctively flick to the dark arch of her left eyebrow in search of the telltale, faintly glowing, lilac "A" that the law made mandatory.

It wasn't there, of course. Androids, even female ones, were around, but they were as expensive to buy and maintain as a privately owned spaceyacht. And just as likely to be out and unattended on a transit world.

My eyes, like those of any photographer, explored the bones of her wrist as she held out her small hand to me. Knowing from their structure, under the real-fur bangle, that the ankles in those pipe-stem boots the women were wearing this season would be well worth the looking at.

"Mi-ister Pike? Mister Eli Pike?"

She spoke hesitantly, the delicacy of her voice matching that of her bones. Her Intragalactic English had an accent I couldn't quite place, yet I sensed in it an echo of a land lying open and prostrate under the heat of a punishing sun.

The fat manager had been right to call her a lady. This was no corridor-walker. And I'd been wrong about the other thing. She had come here looking not for any photographer, but for me. She knew my name.

So why then, all of a sudden, was my scar itching?

I kept my hand away from my head and looked around for the transhaus manager, but he did not seem to be in the room.

"Yes," I said. "I'm Pike."

"Good," she said and smiled. "Could we go somewhere . . . and talk?"

Normally, I could expect the fat manager to be here in his office to give me the receipted bill for my sleep-time. But just because he wasn't, it didn't mean that he couldn't be somewhere outside it with a thick ear pressed close against a thin part of the wall. And if she had something to say that, from the hesitation in her voice, she was in some way not sure of. . . ?

This is where I should have cut out, the way the scar on my head was acting up. But I pressed it hard with my palm, faking the scratching. Don't be silly, I said to myself, and maybe to my scar. If this is the kind of a package they're putting trouble up in these days, where do I line up for my share?

But aloud I said, "I'm . . . I'm just on my way out for something to eat. Would you join me, Miss. . . ?"

She let my question just hang there unanswered. She looked at her wrist-chrono, pushing back the broad bangle with a fingertip.

"Thank you," she said. "But I don't think we have the time. Couldn't ... couldn't we just talk as we walked?"

I shrugged. If she didn't want to be overheard, then just being outside and in motion was of no particular help against anyone even half serious about listening in on what she had to say. But then, maybe on her world directional pickups and tracking equipment were not all that common.

"Fine," I said. "That will be just fine," and I stepped back for her to go out the door before me.

She did, but as she passed the manager's desk I saw her lay two coins on its flat top; heard their dull, plastic click.

Two coins. Double eagles. Forty Earth dollars for what amounted to little more than punching up my name in his computer's "occupied" file? Who needed an itching scar to set his teeth on edge?

I thought to pacify it. Maybe she meant it to cover my bill as well. I'd ask.

My scar wasn't that easy to propitiate. All the same, I followed her out and through the slowly revolving main door of the gasthaus and onto the spaceport perimeter walk, wincing a little as the blistering heat into which we emerged struck me on both cheeks and my eyes.

Chapter Three

Transit worlds, I was beginning to suspect, came in but two varieties. Cold enough to freeze the proverbial nut off its bolt, or hot enough to fry.

Poldrogi was the frying kind, its heat bearable only because of the extreme shortness of its day. It was little more than a place in space where a freighter could warp out long enough to make the planetfall necessary to transship a cargo or to drop off, amid a general shaking of heads, a diehard passenger or two bound for one of the rim worlds.

After all, a man did not head for what the planets closer to the galaxy nucleus called "the home of the loon and the loner" unless he was pretty much one or the other himself, and as if to prove the validity of the self-fulfilling in adages or prophecies or what have you, the rim-worlders were becoming, more or less, a breed unto themselves.

It had seemed to me to be a better place than most to look for the unusual and the unexpected.

The unusual and the unexpected.

Like the booted and fur-bangled figure of the woman walking ahead of me. Her home planet must be a scorching place for her to be so dressed and yet move so lightly in the heavy press of Poldrogi's heat.

I blinked against the glare of the high sun, my eyes watering, and lengthened my stride to overtake her, but she had stopped by the side of a small, dark green and black surface skimmer and was motioning me to slide onto its small double seat.

I hesitated, my head scar itching, and she chose to misinterpret my hanging back.

"I'm sorry," she said. "But the hostel had no cars with air-cooled interiors."

That shouldn't have surprised her and maybe it didn't. When you were an out-of-the-way place like Poldrogi, you had to ship in just about everything you used, and that included a small surface skimmer.

And if you wanted it to reach you in something that resembled a viable lifetime, then you had to span the distances from planet to planet, from star to star, at a rate a great deal better than the speed of light.

That meant the space warp.

That also meant heavy power expenditure even though the warp itself did not seem to go by how physically large an object was, nor how great the distance you wanted to send it. It was the breaking into and the breaking out of the force field that looked to be what ate up all that power.

And that seemed to be a function of the object's mass; its pure weight. A tiny shotgun pellet, for example, needed no more power to be sent to a distant sporting world than did an inflated target marker, if they both weighed the same.

And power, as always, cost.

This didn't mean that the traffic was light; far from it. But it did mean that if your hostel was a cut less than fashionable, you didn't waste your money bringing in something with the weight of a car-cooling unit just in case one of your transients mightn't be willing to take a little of the heat you lived with.

One thing, though, that the weight-power property of the warp did make cheap was the galactic mail.

Half of a planet's daily communications could be, and were, made to fit onto a tissue-thin rectangle of plastic about the size of a man's palm and weighing next to nothing. Flat, automatically guided web containers, weighing as little as the numberless electronic messages packed into them, streamed into and out of asteroid and satellite postal substations.

But straight mail was the only kind of service available at low price. To make a parcel of my camera invited arm-and-leg shipping rates. Yet even a thick sheaf of the holograms that represented the pictures I'd taken with it could be sent anywhere in the galaxy, as a pinpoint-sized pattern of magnetic impulses, for literally the price of a single stamp. And, of course, infinitely faster than any light or radio wave could have carried them.

I shook my head at the woman holding open the skimmer door.

"I'd like to know a little of what you have in mind," I said to her. "After all, I have my license to think of."

This was true, but only partly. How could I tell her that my scar was itching me to the point where the sweat I felt trickling down my sides inside my jumpsuit wasn't all due to Poldrogi's heat?

She looked puzzled. "Your license? To take a picture?"

"No," I said. "I don't need a license to take a picture. I mean my license to carry a camera."

How far out was her native world for her not to know that, since the hard lesson of the Second Police Action, cameras, recorders, transmitters, anything larger than the personal, limited range receivers most people carried, had to be specially licensed? And the licenses, issued by BuPerSec, the Bureau of Personal Security, were almost impossible to get without a Service record to prove your dependability.

Still, the galaxy was some hundred thousand light-years across, and she might really not have heard of a CE license.

Or, more to the point, like most people, although she knew that a camera would record whatever was put in front of it, she just didn't think of one as being a piece of communication equipment.

But fine wrist bones or no, a transit world was no place for a photographer to chance the loss of a license that was a must if he was to ply his trade.

Not that the Poldrogi police could lift mine from me permanently. Experience had taught BuPerSec not to leave *that* potential blackjack to the discretion of any local satrap. But the police of any planet did have the power to impound a man's CE license pending an investigation and a hearing before the Bureau.

And if I'd had the money credits to risk being stranded on a transit world for even a short time without the use of my cameras, I'd be doing my sleeping in a place other than a spaceport transhaus.

Poldrogi was no different from any place that

existed chiefly by catering to people who were just passing through. There is action, there is a ready flow of money credits. But the flow is in the main from transient to local.

And if you happen to be a transient with the bad luck, or the bad judgment, to go broke... ? Well, who can blame the local if he takes it out on you for the slights, the insults, the downright indignities and indecencies he's had to put up with from transients with more money and better brains than to get themselves stranded on his world?

The look on the woman's face was still one of puzzlement, but to my thinking, she'd been holding it too long. She may not have known about a CE license, but she was stalling about something. Something that had brought her to the spaceport transhaus, which she now looked to be groping around for a way to start talking about.

The spaceport transhaus.

The Poldrogi spaceport transhaus.

I slid into the skimmer seat beside her. "Let's go," I said, and added to myself, *before my brains catch up with my head.*

Chapter Four

Poldrogi's fast-moving sun was past its peak, but a full press of heat still burned down on us when Brigit coasted her skimmer to a stop and we lost the breeze of our motion. Despite my misgivings, the assignment, as she'd explained it to me on the way to the Home, seemed harmless enough. All she wanted me to do was to photograph her husband, Anton Plagiar, while he put on a magic show for the orphans living at the Home.

A woven-reed fence, shoulder high, and through its broad opened gates, a scrubby lawn swarming with children, all yelling and shouting. And beyond them the flat, one-story baked-mud-brick building of the Home itself.

Bushes, dry and stunted looking, cluttered the area close up to the Home and were scattered in clumps about the crowded lawn, their only effect being to emphasize the burned-out look of the place. Twilight couldn't come any too soon on a world like this.

In the middle of the alleged lawn and all the furor, there floated, about a yard-and-a-half off the ground, a circular platform, and when I saw it I nodded my approval.

Long ago, when I was only a little bigger than these children noisily scrambling all around Brigit and me, magic had been a pretty serious interest with me, and it pleased me to see the mark of a man who knew what he was about. There is nothing like open space under a performer's stage to put things like trapdoors or hidden assistants out of the audience's mind.

I felt a hand placed lightly on my arm and looked down to see Brigit smiling up at me. She said something, but I couldn't make it out over all that childish din. I held up a hand, found a small pebble at my feet, and tossed it under the floating platform.

To hold a stage up off the ground with ordinary hover units was, of course, out of the question the way their blast churned up the dust and debris and everything else in their path. But you could use the new miniaturized antigrav units, or you could just let the stage sit on posts and a solid base and mask the view with the crisscrossing rays of dozens of tiny refraction units.

Either way, the units not only cost the proverbial satchelful of credits but took a high degree of technical competence to set up.

The arcing path of the pebble I'd thrown glowed faintly blue for a brief moment and I knew that Plagiar was using antigrav units and that his under-platform space was really empty of hiding places.

"You are a man of no small curiosity," Brigit laughed when we were free of the press of the midget crowd and I could hear her. And on her the tiny mustache of sweat beading her upper lip looked good.

Nosy would have been a better word for her to have used, but I didn't correct her. I'd just noticed, at the X-braced wood door of the pressed-down-looking main building, a cluster of three or four men in ordinary blue and yellow business tunics. Compactly built, all young, all tough looking, and they seemed to suddenly be very interested in me. In me, or in me and Brigit hanging from my arm.

I must have hesitated in my stride, because I felt Brigit's hand on my arm give it a little tug and she led me right up the single broad step flanked by the scrubby plantings and toward the staring group.

Philanthropist her husband might be, and here to give a few moments of pleasure to some unfortunate children, but I knew a phalanx of bodyguards from a group of ordinary plainclothes police when I saw one and, for that matter, so did my scar. But with Brigit on my right arm and my camera off its strap around my neck and in my left hand, there wasn't much I could do but let it itch.

We went up to and past the squat phalanx, they tracking us with their heads and eyes as we moved.

At the last possible moment, one of them leaned forward and I braced myself, for what I didn't really know, but he only hooked a thick finger over the outside latch of the door and pulled it open for us.

"Thank you," I said, and when I looked back over my shoulder for the answer I did not hear him give, a strangeness in the look of the closing door nudged at my consciousness.

A strangeness that made it all the way and brought me up to turn and stare to be sure that I'd seen aright.

I had.

In this strange place, the front door seemed to have no knob ... nor any other way of opening it from the inside that I could see.

Chapter Five

I felt a light touch on my arm that took me away from my contemplation of the knobless door. It was Brigit and she was beckoning for me to bring my face down close to hers.

"Please do not mention that I found you in a gasthaus," she whispered.

That surprised me a little. If she'd known to ask for me by name, why should she now be shy about the kind of place in which she'd come upon me?

Then I smiled to myself. That was my ego nudging me. It should have remembered that she probably hadn't asked the gasthaus manager for Eli Pike, but for a photographer and his register that identified me as such, would have my name for him to give her as well.

I looked down into her upturned face, ready to quip an inane "I won't if you won't" but her eyes were turned from mine and intent on the closed panels of a sliding door one side of which one of the thickset young men was pressing open.

I followed her into a surprisingly small room for so broad an entry. Or maybe it was just the forceful presence I sensed emanating from the man I took to be Anton Plagiar that seemed to fill it and give that impression.

Hard was not the word to describe the look of his face. Driving was not it either. Yet I had the feeling of looking at a man who was capable of exerting great pressure if it moved him to do so.

Inside, I shrugged. A man did not get to have the financial stature he appeared to have without having some look of tautness about him. Or maybe it was just the natural keying up of a performer before he went into his act. After all, Brigit *had* told me that they'd more or less just arrived on Poldrogi and already he was about to perform for its children.

Physically, Anton Plagiar was a small man with thick white hair built high on his head and a thin white mustache to go with it. I hadn't given any thought to how old a man he might be although, after seeing Brigit, I might have expected him to be much younger.

He was as compactly put together as any of his bodyguards, the way I'd noticed the rim-world people seemed in the main to be. But I suppose they couldn't help but grow that way in places where livable space and food were anything but easy to come by. Planets that often had the pull of heavy gravity to thicken their denizens' bones.

But the electric-blue evening tights and waist length silver jacket he wore had not come from the shop of any mass sale house. And I would have bet that never in his life had a provincial tailor gotten his hands on material that could drape like that.

He was practicing a standard card retrieval from the apparently empty air when we came in, showing his hand empty in between with a credible front-and-back palm. Warming up for his performance, I took it.

He continued for a moment longer before he handed his cards to the bully boy who'd slid open the door for us and came forward. He did not wait for Brigit to introduce us but held out a hand that looked like a pink claw. "You are?" he said.

I switched my camera to my left hand before I took his in mine. It felt as horny and dry as I'd expected. "Pike," I said. "Eli Pike."

I do not like people to press my hand harder than I feel they need to, nor do I like them to take hold of my elbow when they do so.

Plagiar did both. "Yes. You are the photographer. Come."

He attempted to guide me farther into the room toward the small taboret set to one side of the room's single broad window. "There are some things you need to know about photographing a magic act if you are to shoot mine so that you do not reveal its secrets."

I stood my ground. In a moment Plagiar released his grip on my hand and arm, looking at Brigit as he did so. I noticed that her eyes did not waver from his.

I stretched out my free hand and took a single card from the pack Plagiar had handed his bully boy. I made it vanish into the air, showed the back of my hand empty, the palm also, brought the card back with a small snap. My front-and-back palm was superior to his, the movement natural and easy, as it should have been. There had been a time when my living depended on my skill with magic.

I handed the card back to Plagiar's man, resisting the temptation to take the pack from his hand and mix it back in with a one-handed shuffle. "I think you can trust me to know what to shoot and what not to," I said.

Plagiar's answer was a throaty grunt. I took it to be one of approval. It may not have been. Few men of power like to be topped—or that anyone should presume to do so as openly as I had. It did not matter to me. That it should not was a major reason why I'd chosen to be a free-lancer.

Plagiar turned from me and now that he no longer commanded my attention, I became aware of others in the room; of the young men scattered about it, all conservatively dressed in blue and yellow, until the ordinary business tunics began to look to me like some sort of unobtrusive uniform.

I also became aware that Brigit had slid open the door to what looked like a small study and was taking my camera from my hand. I didn't want to let it go, but I supposed that with all of the bully boys that seemed to be thronging the place, it would be more than well guarded if left beside Brigit's shoulder purse on the low bench this side of the study door.

"A small drink," she said, "while we wait." Sure enough, gazing past her into the shaded chamber, I saw, on a low table in front of a narrow divan, glasses and a tall, cool-looking bottle that made my mouth water just to look at it.

I never got the chance to find out if it tasted the way it looked. Brigit had scarcely settled us on the divan and was starting to fuss with the glasses when the door she'd slid closed behind her opened and a bully boy stuck in his head.

He spoke with the same strange accent that Brigit

had, but heavier by far. His message was plain enough, though.

The master wanted me on stage and ready when he made his entrance, and that was right now.

I sighed, disentangled my long legs from each other and from those of the divan table, and followed the bully boy. Absently I noticed, when I scooped up my camera, that it felt vaguely strange in my hand. I glanced at it, but there was no mistaking its larger-than-standard size, the special pic-hold finder. It was my camera all right.

There was a flurry of activity going on in the main hall as I passed through it. Two of the bully boys had long red capes over their shoulders, the hoods thrown back. One of them was fiddling with a glowing, lilac "A" on the tip of one finger; the other had already pasted his over his left eyebrow and was patting it more firmly in place with a stubby middle finger.

I grinned to myself. Androids. There was a law in the galaxy, heavily enforced, that an android had to wear his telltale badge, fitted to him when he was made, so that a human would not be deceived by a resemblance that, with high-grade work, was often impossible to detect by the unaided eye or touch.

But no one had thought it necessary to pass a law that a man couldn't masquerade as an android, so there were no such regulations on any planet that I knew of. Plagiar wouldn't be the first magician to outfit his assistants to look like something more glamorous than simple humans.

Right now, because of their rarity and high cost, androids were both glamorous and objects of great curiosity. One would have been a rarity. Two, on the same stage with him, would give Plagiar's act a decided fillip.

Plagiar, himself, was busy fitting the loose hood of the red cloak he, too, had donned over his white hair and down to shield his face.

My grin broadened when I saw that. Three men, all looking the same, I was sure, would follow me out to the floating platform.

"Do not begin until I give you a signal." It was Brigit, who had come out of the small study and now seemed to be headed away from us toward the back of the building.

I nodded, smiling. I was almost certain what Plagiar's opening effect was going to be.

At the blank front door the bully boy stopped and slapped a palm against its heavy panel. It was opened for him, in a moment, by one of the bully boys outside.

Is there no way out of this place from the inside? I thought of safety and fire regulations, but the arms of the galaxy spiral spread wide and Poldrogi is a remote planet.

"There," said the bully boy guiding me. He pointed at the circular stage floating poised in the air at the center of the lawn and surrounded by a mass of waiting children. "You go, and you wait."

I went, and I was ready to wait.

Chapter Six

A yard-and-a-half off the ground, Plagiar's performing stage floated about chest-high to me. When I managed to press my way through the chattering, laughing mass of children that circled it, I could see that it was now rotating slowly, giving the spiral pattern of magenta and yellow on its floor an almost hypnotic quality.

I shook my head, blinked my eyes. With that device, he took care of anyone seeing a trapdoor or any other kind of opening in the stage floor.

I leaned down to peer under the platform, steadying myself with one hand on its edge as I did so.

Firm. The platform was not only firm, but my hand felt as though there was a hidden pressure pushing against its weight.

Gyros. To the antigrav units holding his stage clear of the ground, Plagiar had added an internal system of gyroscopes to keep it steady against the notoriously bouncy feel of shifting weight pressures. He must have a potful of money or the men working for him to set up this platform were technical geniuses—maybe both. Yet I'd never so much as heard of him.

The platform was thin at its edge, no more than four inches, I guessed. But it thickened toward its center, so gradually that the foot or so depth it had at that point was difficult to see even when you knew it had to be there and were looking for it as I was.

I straightened. Wait. Plagiar's man had said to wait.

I looked around for Brigit, wanting to locate her now so that I'd know where to look for her signal to start shooting when her husband came on stage.

I couldn't find her. Then, out of the corner of my eye, I caught a movement at the top of the Home building. It was Brigit, waving to me. She was at a corner of the roof, behind a waist-high parapet. It was a logical enough vantage spot from which to watch her husband's performance, even though it did mean she would be out in the raw heat of the sun.

But then, even with the bushes, there was no more real shade down here than there was up there, and the roof at least had the illusion of airiness.

I waved back to her and then saw that her motion was really a signal. She wanted me up on the stage?

I pointed to myself and to the stage and saw her nod.

I'd covered many shows, presentations, speeches, but always from audience level or unobtrusively from the wings. No performer I'd ever worked with had wanted a photographer onstage during his act, diverting the audience's attention away from him.

But she was Plagiar's wife and she should certainly know how he wanted himself covered.

I shrugged, set my camera on the platform, noting once again its strange feel, and clambered up after it.

There was a blare of trumpets, from where I could not at once tell, and then I found the sound was coming from under my feet. Speakers, in the platform, of course.

The babble of the children stopped for a moment, and then their treble voices broke out in a shout of anticipation.

I turned and saw three red-cloaked figures, their long garb trailing the ground, seemingly floating toward us.

They circled the platform once, twice, then vaulted lightly onto it and dropped down at once to become three brooding hooded figures hunched at equal distances along its perimeter. None of them had come anywhere close to the center of the platform.

I watched the area at the center of the spiral, my eyes squinting down, guarding against what I knew had to come. Atop the platform I moved with the pattern so that, for me, it had lost whatever hypnotic effect it might have had.

From under my feet, a crescendo of sound and then the expected flash. The flash of bright light and the billow of colorful smoke and, in its midst when it cleared, arms spread wide, the white-haired, mustached figure in electric-blue and silver.

I did not need to look at Brigit to know that there was no point in photographing this sudden apparition. It looked like Anton Plagiar, it was meant to, but it wasn't Anton Plagiar.

This was the man who had borne the heat and discomfort of being penned up in the compartment hidden in the platform's foot-thick center since it had first been set up, perhaps hours earlier. It was a centuries-old technique for a magical appearance, and the gasp it brought from the audience of children showed that it was still as effective as it had ever been.

And now the tempo of the music coming from the platform's hidden speakers picked up. The three red-hooded figures rose and began to glide along the edge of the platform with their peculiar flowing gait.

Gliding and circling, raising and lowering their bodies; swifter and swifter grew their pace, tighter and tighter their circling path, passing first on one side of me and then on the other.

And the Anton-double was waving his arms and then, suddenly, to the accompaniment of another gasp from the gathered children, in each of his hands out of nowhere was a glowing wand streaming a banner of yellow-and-magenta to match the spiral of the platform floor.

About his head and body he waved them; their streamers swirling and spiraling, the red-clad figures gliding and circling.

Into the air he threw the wands. Straight up and with a mighty heave.

High they rose. Higher and higher with all eyes following their soaring path.

Mine included.

Then I caught myself and snapped my eyes back to the center of the stage where the three red figures, their cloaks billowing, had converged upon and were swirling about the one electric-blue-and-silver clad one.

And I knew that when the soaring banners fell back to the stage the Anton-double would be inside one of the hooded red cloaks and the man who stepped forward to catch them and go on with the show would be the real Anton Plagiar, the Anton Plagiar I'd been hired to cover.

I brought my camera up to the ready, to catch the first of my pictures as he did so.

I brought my camera up and the strangeness of its feel in my hands almost forced its way into the forefront of my consciousness.

Almost, but not quite. Yet, just as a craftsman can pick up a tool from a benchful of others looking exactly like it and know it to be his own, so my hands felt in my camera a strangeness as I lifted it up to my face.

On the rim of my vision I saw a movement and looking, saw Brigit waving, frantically it seemed to me, from her vantage point on the roof.

I looked with my eyes and my mind, but my hands moved on their own in a pattern set by long habit.

Down they pointed the camera and they squeezed its release.

Once, they squeezed it to check its operation against the strangeness of the heft they sensed. Downward, to keep the flash of even my low-intensity and relatively safe laser light from needlessly striking the eyes of my subject.

Once, they squeezed, and I was staggered.

Under my feet the platform shuddered and dipped and, whirring through the space my head had just dropped away from, was a sound I hadn't heard since the Second Peace Action.

I heard the thin, almost inaudible passage of the masher beam from a sniper's weapon. Had it even so much as brushed my skull, the bone-conducted vibrations would have homogenized my brain and I would have been dead even before my body could begin to fall.

But even with the near-miss, my head hummed with the passage of its peripheral shock wave and my reflexes were numbed to the point where I could not fully control my body.

But numbed reflexes or no, my body remembered its combat-learned lessons and started to drop me flat to the floor of the now tilting and lurching stage.

As I went down I saw, following the pointing of my camera in my hands, still nosed downward, a snaking, living gash forming itself in the garish pattern of the platform floor.

In a flash of understanding as brilliant as only hindsight can be, I knew the reason for the feel of strangeness my camera had.

Someone—and he could have had the chance only while my camera was out of my sight during the few moments it rested on the low bench beside Brigit's purse—had removed the heart unit from my relatively safe photographic laser and slipped into its holding clip a focused, high-intensity killer unit.

This was not a particularly startling devising. After all, hadn't the original laser used for its light source a photographic flashtube?

But killer units operated in microsecond bursts of infrared light. *This* beam was continuous and, squeeze my release as hard as my masher-beam-stunned reflexes would let me, *I couldn't shut it off*.

And *that* was startling. A man who could put together a high-intensity, sustained-energy exciter and its power supply, and do it compactly enough to add almost undetectable ounces to the weight of my camera, had a frightening degree of technical competence, that, if nothing else, bordered on the near-miraculous.

And I sincerely did not know if I marveled more at this than I did at his, or their, audacity in using so hoary a dodge as hiding a weapon in a camera; a dodge that, except for my hands' animal sense in detecting the strange feel of the camera they held, might have worked—perhaps because of its very hoariness.

Judging by the platform's mad pitching and rolling, the slashing, snaking laser must be playing havoc with the antigrav units holding the stage up, the gyros straining to keep it level.

Now I consciously fought my own beam-weakened hands to keep the camera from slipping out of their grip. Fought to hold it and keep it pointed downward and away from the now roiling, screaming mass of children around me.

Fighting the laser beam, and swearing at the animals—the unfeeling beasts—who, to kill a man, would choose a time and a weapon that, like a hose that could not be turned off, would spray its death at the youngsters pressing close around him.

Chapter Seven

I hit the ground rolling, flung there partly by the pitching and tilting of the platform, partly by my own badly coordinated efforts to escape.

Over and around me now was the obscene-sounding blat of a police stun-gun firing; the Home's own guard, perhaps. I felt a sudden wetness on my ear and neck but I did not reach up my hand to see if I had been hit.

My camera was under me; I'd managed that in my falling. Flat, pointing downward, its hellish laser boring into the ground.

The children, at least, were safe from it and whoever came to retrieve it should, after what had happened, have enough sense to approach it with caution.

I could not run; my stunned nerves would not direct my legs to a proper rising sequence.

I rolled. Like a giant, elongated tumbleweed before a hot wind of panic, I rolled. Rolled for the shelter of the scrawny bushes pressing against the base of the Home building.

It saved me. That, and the masking confusion of screaming children. Rolling, I was flat to the ground and I suppose they expected to see the running figure I'd tried to be except that my knees wouldn't lift me.

A running figure . . . and one going *away* from the area.

I rolled toward its center, thinking not of the guards or the crowd, but of the sniper. From the direction of the house he'd fired, and but the one time. High, he seemed to be, and my instinct was to get in under his gun, below his line of fire.

Into the bushes I rolled, snaking between them and the dusty wall of the building.

I lay panting, shaking my head although I knew that would be no help in clearing it of the shock wave-induced hum.

I had never before been hit by the shock wave that traveled, like a hard, invisible funnel, on the periphery of a masher beam. And, from the feel it it, this one time was enough for me.

Experimentally, I flexed my fingers. Their strength did not seem to be merely diminished, but also came and went, came and went, like the phasing of a sound wave.

There was a weakness . . . and then a slow building to what seemed like normal strength . . . and then the weakness . . . and the strengthening again.

My hearing . . . my vision . . . both seemed to ebb and flow . . . ebb and flow . . . following the same unsettling pattern.

I peered as best I could up the low front of the building, searching for the sniper.

Leaning over the parapet, scanning the bushes that half-hid me, was Brigit. Then, at least, the sniper hadn't been on the roof, else she would have seen him.

But maybe he was, and maybe she had. Was she with me or had she set me up to kill her husband, then be knocked off myself before I could defend or explain myself? Explain myself, with the transhaus manager to back at least that part of my story, that it was she who had sought me out, and that I'd never even seen her husband before now, much less had a motive to murder him.

But what if she were as innocent of intent to kill as I; wasn't just another young wife with a sniper boyfriend and an urge to nudge an aging husband out of the triangle?

She could clear me ... and completely.

The sky behind Brigit had grown less eyeball-searing. Poldrogi's quick sun was not yet low, but it was getting there. I peered up at her as well as my phasing eyes and the thin bramble-branches would let me.

The laser killer.

There was the killer laser in my camera. Had she provided the opportunity for it to be installed on purpose?

She needn't have. You could build the laser then, knowing of Brigit's propensity for having her husband photographed for her scrapbook, simply wait for the opportunity to insert it into some unsuspecting photographer's camera. It could just have happened to be me. It *had* happened to be me.

Men and women were mingled with the quieting children now, leading some out and away through the open gate, herding others toward the Home, and toward me, hidden in the sparse growth at the base of its facade.

And there were those among the new arrivals who stood or ran, shouting, still seeking me, still circling the grounds; the now sagged-to-the-dirt platform.

Plagiar was not in sight, nor were his bully boys.

Brigit. Dare I risk showing myself to her hoping that she could make it down to me, to intercede for me ... to explain?

Or, if I did, would she shout and point me out to those who were hunting me and let the mob perhaps do for her what the sniper's beam hadn't been able to?

I peered up at her leaning out over the parapet and mentally I flipped a coin again and again. Dare I trust her, or dare I not?

And then I laughed and the mental coin stood on its edge. There was no need for me to risk my life on a wrong decision. All I had to do was to wait until I could hear what story she told the police I knew must soon respond to the crowd's clamor, if they weren't already on the way.

If she cleared me, I could emerge from hiding. If she had her own tale to tell ... at least I'd know where I stood in *that* quarter.

Hide, until I could hear a newscast or see a newsfax.

Hide, but not here. The cover was thin and the police would search the grounds as a matter of routine.

Get away, but how?

On moonless Poldrogi, with its short, short day, night fell almost as rapidly as pulling down a shade, but I could not wait for its cover.

I could not wait, period.

Among the men gathering on the Home lawn were those who wore jumpsuits and coveralls not unlike the one I had on. Perhaps if I emerged and moved about purposefully, pretended to be one of them, looking for myself? After all, how many of them had been here to see me on the platform and so could recognize me now? Very few, if any at all, now that Plagiar and his bully boys had vanished.

And to be caught in the act of hiding would, in itself, be damning identification.

I had no real choice but to try to brazen it out. It was either that or take to my heels in headlong flight, and, by this action, betray myself to the gathering crowd.

I waited for a rising phase in the unnerving ebb and flow of my strength and when it came, I took a deep, wavering breath, raised myself up ... and stepped as casually as I could out of the shadow of the bushes and onto the lawn.

A shout, a pointing ... and a surge of the crowd in my direction.

But I had seen it for myself and was already running.

Running as only the desperate can run.

Running for the all-encompassing fence. Running and praying that the strength of my legs, my body, my hands, would not fail me, abandon me to the thing I heard finding its voice behind me.

My neck, my shoulder, the side of my head. The feeling of wetness I'd felt strike at them. The stungun. Its charge had not hit me, but its projectile had been from a riot shell.

A riot shell, designed to not only stun the man it struck, but to spray and splash his companions around him with a telltale dye so that for forty-eight hours, at least, no matter how they ran, how they tried to blend with the innocents about them, they could not conceal from a seeking eye the guilty fact of their presence on the scene.

My shoulder, my neck, my head ... they glowed in the lowering angle of the sun with a green so vivid it was almost audible.

I am not an athlete, I have never been, but my urgency lifted me over the fence and into the scrubby brush beyond it.

I ran. Swearing at the brambles that would catch and hold me back. Swearing at the assassin who would make of me a tool. Swearing most of all at myself for not heeding the warning of my scar when first I set eyes on Brigit ... first heard her speak to me in her oddly accented voice.

I ran, dodging, falling, changing my direction, hearing the sounds of pursuit grow and diminish and sweating out the nerve-stretching strain of not knowing if they were really falling behind me or if it was just my own flawed hearing playing me false.

I ran, evading yet never losing my pursuers, until I stumbled, in the at-last-fallen darkness, into the black and weed-dotted waters of a Poldrogi lake.

Chapter Eight

I sat, over my head in black water, breathing through a reed, feeling the ooze of the lake bottom beneath me sucking at me; feeling the unsettling bump and nudge of night-blinded things slithering against me.

I sat, waiting for those who would make me their prey to tire of the hunt.

Tire, not enough to abandon their searching for me, I could not hope for that. To them, I was a would-be killer, and vicious.

Vicious and callous, to place their children in so terrible a danger. Their determination to seize me was, I was certain, as great as mine would have been had I been in their place; had it been a child of mine so placed in jeopardy.

But they would tire enough, I hoped, to be for the moment satisfied with the setting up of a guard and the waiting out of the night that, on their moonless planet, was shorter even than the time of their daylight.

A letting up of vigilance that might give me the slim edge I needed to evade them completely, or at least until the telltale dye lost its green glow ... or I could learn how Brigit meant to tell her story.

Around me, the water churned up by the blast from the crossing and recrossing hover-craft had let up its tugging at me. They might still be aloft, their heat-detectors dangling, but if they were, they had at least shifted their operations away from the weeds in which I was hiding.

Cautiously, I raised myself up, rocking a little to break the sucking grip of the mud that held me, until my head was clear enough of the water's surface for me to listen.

From across the lake came the sound of hover-craft beating.

Good. For that much, then, I could be thankful. They were now searching to find me on the far shore which I probably would have struck out for had I been able to swim.

But I couldn't swim, so I was still on the same side of the lake as when I'd plunged into it. A hard fact I was hoping would escape the thinking of my pursuers.

Slowly, keeping my ear on the high sound of raised voices as best as my phasing hearing would let me, and using it as a guide, I groped along the lake bottom with feet I could not fully trust to have the strength to hold me, the full sense of feel to guide me.

Breathing through my reed where the water was so deep as to close over my head; slithering on my stomach and hands where it wasn't, I made my way along the shore, expecting at any moment to hear a rousing shout of discovery, feel the stupefying blast of a stun-gun, or the knifing slash of a pistol's laser.

And at long last, the voices in my ear were faint,

even when my hearing reached a high point in its ebb and flow.

In toward the shore I turned. In toward the faintly blacker mass the scrubby undergrowth made against the starshine that was the only relief from darkness Poldrogi's moonless night afforded.

In I moved, until the upward slope of the rock-studded bank was unmistakable, the water frothing lightly against my ankles.

Up the bank I staggered, falling forward onto it with something akin to a gasp of relief, in spite of its sharp and craggy feel.

I did not hear him approach. In the blackness I certainly did not see him.

Face down, I felt only the hard pressure of his weapon on the back of my skull; heard only his voice, flat and quiet in my ear.

"Freeze," he said.

I froze.

Chapter Nine

"Piot Kval," the man behind the battered wood desk said in his heavy Poldrogi accent.

His uniform tunic was open at the neck and mottled to a dark brown with sweat. In his hand he held a self-contained power fan larger than any I'd seen before, and he was making no progress at all with it on the sweat that beaded his red face and bald head. If he'd used a mirror instead, his eyes would have run a frost line wherever they touched.

I stared at him.

Stared at him and my camera on the desktop in front of him.

My camera. Clean and undamaged and looking as though I'd never crushed it to the earth beneath my body; as though it had never held any laser but the one in its own innocuous speedlight.

"Piot Kval," he repeated and waited for my answer.

I shook my head. "I don't know the name," I said. And I didn't.

"You do not know the name," he said. He reached out to his desk, picked up my wallet from the small array of my possessions spread out beside my camera; a scattering of keys, coins, pocket flotsam, my sleeve camera, kept safe from the cold Poldrogi lake by its waterproof casing.

Slowly, almost lazily, using only his one hand, the other not putting down his fan, he examined his prize, fingering the few plastic credits in their separate compartment, idly turning over the leaves of the card section.

Without saying a word, he was putting a chill in the air.

I pulled closer about me the thin blanket the police had given me while they went over my sodden jumpsuit and boots. It reeked of disinfectant, but it was better than standing before the police corporal in nothing but my skin.

My head and neck still glowed a bright green, I knew. They had done nothing about the riot marker dye I was stained with. My beam-shocked strength still came and went. I fought myself to keep it from showing.

I knew what the cold-eyed corporal was looking for, and I was sure he knew I knew. Yet when he came to it he flicked right on past it and, if he wanted my heart to skip a beat, it did.

He flicked the small panel over, then flicked it back, as though he'd just that moment noticed what it held.

He pressed open the clear plastic envelope shape, inserted a heavy thumb, sat there, not pulling out the yellow plastic rectangle, not taking his thumb from it.

He looked up at me. "You gave us a great deal of trouble, you know," he said. "It was all my men could do to keep our people from overtaking you."

If he meant to sweat me, he was doing it. I

couldn't help licking my lips. "Thank you," I said, and I think I might have meant it.

I couldn't take my eyes off his thumb on my Communications Equipment license.

Ebb and flow went my strength. Ebb and flow.

"There are no thanks required," he said, speaking in the same matter-of-fact manner as had the fat transhaus manager when he'd turned aside my thanks for calling me to what I'd thought was a photo assignment. "If we had tried to save you from them openly, our on-site people might have resisted our efforts and it would have caused embarrassment all around. It is better that they should believe for a while that they lost you themselves."

He ran his thumb back and forth over the face of my CE license. If he meant to remind me that he could pull it, he didn't have to. "Would it make a difference if I told you your fingerprint had not yet been obliterated from the record?" he said.

I didn't follow him. I didn't follow anything. My camera, battered, perhaps even damaged where someone had smashed it open to get at its killer laser, would have been a starting point for me to at least begin to tell my story.

My camera, clean and pristine looking on the corporal's desk. What could I say that it didn't give the lie to before I opened my mouth?

I was staring at it and now I saw the corporal eyeing it with a flicker of interest.

"Look," I said, taking the plunge. "Am I being charged with anything specific?"

The corporal's eyebrows went up. "Specific? A charge?" He smiled, but his eyes did not warm, and neither did he take his thumb from my CE license. "You feel a guilt, perhaps? You must remember that you ran."

I ran," I said. "I heard a masher beam, I got sprayed with riot dye, and the mob took off after me. I ran. I ran as hard as I could."

I did not mention that my head had not let up its humming since the near-miss passage of the beam, nor that the phasing in and out of my strength was just on the rim of my control. I did not mention this because what I wanted was out, and not to be held even for medical observation.

But if the corporal did not finish with me soon, I knew the wavelike surging would slip beyond my control and be as evident to him, and anyone else within spraying distance, as would be the effect of the surging on my tired and queasy stomach.

"A masher beam," the corporal was saying. "You are familiar with the sound of a sniper's weapon?"

"Look among the cards in your hand," I said. "You'll find my SpaceNav discharge. I'm familiar with the sound of a sniper's weapon."

"Yes. And yet is it not most curious? A weapon capable of firing a masher beam ... at a children's home? You could not have been mistaken about the sound? A flying insect perhaps? Coming at a critical moment?"

His thumb did not move from my CE license. And from his tone I couldn't tell if I was the only one to have heard the beam ... or if he even believed what I'd said.

Believe what I said? He had the look of a man from whom you'd just taken a big pot asking to see your openers.

I touched a hand to the dye on my head. "This

is no mistake; it set me up for the crowd. And something was going on to get them riled up."

He was silent for a long moment, the only sound in the room being that of my own breath in my nostrils and the faint whir of his fan.

Abruptly he pulled his thumb clear of my CE license, spread my wallet on the desktop in front of him. "These," he said, jabbing at my license with a thick forefinger. "These they do not hand out without some discretion. The fact that you are the possessor of an authentic one . . ."

An authentic one! Then the corporal had checked it out more thoroughly than his casual manner with it had indicated.

". . . would indicate that you are a man of some dependability."

He folded over my wallet, leaned back in his chair. "Mr. Pike," he said, "I can tell you that the dye on your head was not fired at you by any of my men. It could be a . . . a joke of practicality, or it could be that someone has designs upon you.

He eyed me a moment. "It could also be that you have not wished to confide in me . . . that you are involved in something you do not wish to speak of to the police. . . ."

He let his voice trail off and then, after a long moment in which I did not pick up on his silence, he raised it. "Kuba," he called, and, when a sweating police private came in through the door behind me, "please see to it that the dye on Mr. Pike's head is neutralized and that his things are returned to him."

He was no longer looking at me and his voice sounded disinterested. Was he turning me loose? It sounded like it.

I pointed to my camera and my things on the desk. "Could I take these with me now?" I asked.

"If you wish," the corporal said. "Kuba will have a receipt for you to sign."

When I hefted my camera, I knew I'd been right. Its feel in my hand now was as it should have been. I was sure that when I got the chance to look, I'd find no killer laser, no beautifully miniaturized power pack.

I followed the private.

"Kuba," the corporal's voice came after us, "when he is ready, drive Mr. Pike wherever he wishes to go."

He was turning me loose, and with few questions. Why?

I turned in the doorway. "Thank you," I started to say, then, remembering the local reaction to thanks, stopped myself in the middle of the phrase.

The corporal looked up. "Yes?"

"I . . . this Piot Kval, am I supposed to know him?" I said.

"It is of no consequence," the corporal said. "If the name is not known to you, it is not known to you."

His voice was an unmistakable dismissal and I took the hint, even though I felt uneasy. I thought of it, but I did not search my clothes for hidden carrier-beam transmitters when Kuba brought them to me, clean and dry.

"My wrist-chrono," I said. "I had a wrist-chrono."

Kuba tapped my sleeve pocket and, when I groped in it, my fingers touched my timepiece.

"Thank you," I said without thinking.

"Thanks are not necessary," Kuba said, but I was already nodding that I knew.

He left me and I was glad to be alone to struggle with my clothes and my great weariness.

Piot Kval, I thought to myself as I waited for a rise in the strength of my hands. My clothes were clean, and they were dry. But they were also stiffened and rough and they smelled highly of the ever-present Poldrogi disinfectant.

Piot Kval. And the corporal with the cold eyes seemed to feel that I ought to know him.

Piot Kval . . . and my fingerprints on a record.

No, not fingerprints, finger*print*.

Fingerprint! And I had an idea.

Finger*print!*

A great wave of queasiness surged up. I fought it down. Rest. I needed rest.

Rest . . . and sleep . . . and a chance for my body to clear itself of shock . . . to stop this dreadful hum piercing my head. . . .

I dressed, and when I was ready, went looking for Kuba and the promised ride home.

Home. The transhaus and its sleep cubicle . . . and my thumb*print* on the safebox at the foot of my bunk.

I might have been wrong, my hearing at a low point, but I was sure the corporal had said "print" and not "prints." And the transhaus was the only place that I knew had required a record of just my one thumbprint.

Not as a record in itself, but as a pattern for the safebox lock to record electronically, and to recognize when it was presented to it again by the simple act of my pressing my thumb against its lockplate.

It was at least a starting point, but it would have to wait.

Wait . . . and sleep first . . . and where was Kuba? Ah, Kuba.

I was proud of the way I could walk without weaving . . . and I resented his hand under my arm.

I yanked my arm away from his support. "I'm all right," I said.

"Yes," he said. "There is a step here . . . and another below that and then we are on the level ground."

I did not thank him.

Weave . . . do not weave when you walk . . . tired . . . else they will keep you . . . must not let them keep you.

The hum . . . the hum drilling in my head. The masher beam, maybe closer than I thought. . . .

Chapter Ten

I stood on the broad, single step that led up to the transhaus entrance and watched the twin green taillights of the police car skim away from me and get smaller and smaller as they got closer and closer together.

I shook my head—a reflex response to the phasing—and as I turned they were waiting for me. Two of them, stepping from the shadow at one side of the slowly revolving door.

I blinked at them. They were familiar, yet I'd never seen them before. Of that I was sure.

The hard pressure on my ribs as they came up on either side of me was familiar, too ... and that I *had* felt before.

The taller one's weapon, pointed at me, even through a pocket, should have made me afraid.

But it didn't. What I felt was a great weariness and a kind of sad indignation at being put upon for so long, being kept from the rest I'd earned and wanted so badly.

He was taller than his friend, but still short compared to my six-feet-four. He was young, he was tough, and he was expecting no trouble from me.

I was vastly weary and I was filling up with indignation. In what felt like a kind of syrupy slow motion I turned into him and away from his buddy on my other side.

In turning, my size thirteen foot came down on his foot and pinned it to the ground so that he could not step away from me.

Had the light been better, I'm sure I would have been very interested in watching my two hands grip the barrel of his weapon through the cloth of his pocket, and twist.

Twist outward, in a way that his fingers could not bend. Or maybe they could be made to at that. His yelp in my ears was only a kind of obbligato to the snap I heard, muted, of course, that seemed to go with the loosening of his grip.

But the light was good enough for me to see my left hand slide along his right arm and into his pocket and emerge, slightly sticky and red-bedaubed, with a stubby handgun.

My hand and the gun did not stop moving. Idly, I watched their slow progress upward, upward until the gun rested under the young man's chin.

It rested, or at least it looked to me like it did, but I could have been wrong because his head raised up and the gun slid on past his lip and nose.

Red again. On the chin, on the lip, on the nose. But color is hard to tell in dim light. It could be brown ... or even green. No, I had a feeling for color. My first impression had been that it was red. I'd stay with that. Red.

Tired. He seemed suddenly to be as tired as I was. His eyes closed very slowly, the dark pupils rolling upward and back, so that only the whites were left for the heavy lids to slip down over.

He floated. Like a huge toy settling to the bottom of a child's play pool he settled to the transhaus step.

His weapon was still in my hand. I stared at it. Red. It was red all right, and I felt a glow of pleasure warming me. It was nice to know that you could trust your first impression to be right ... especially about a thing that mattered in your work. Color. A sense of color *is* important to a photographer in his work.

I stared at the gun, kept staring, trying to think what I could possibly want with it. My eyes followed along its barrel, outward, upward ... and I was looking at the young man's friend.

He had his right hand inside his tunic front and he seemed to be frozen in that position.

I made a little circle with his friend's gunpoint, chiefly to reassure him that my first flush of indignation at being kept from a well-deserved rest was over. I was sorry, of course, but he could see my point, couldn't he?

He said nothing and then I realized that I hadn't either. I'd been doing all my talking in my head.

But his hand was coming out very slowly from the front of his tunic.

His tunic. Now I knew why he and his friend had looked familiar at first sight. It was blue and yellow.

A blue and yellow business tunic. Plagiar's colors. Of course, he and his friend were two of Anton Plagiar's bully boys ... and I'd treated them very shabbily.

His hand was free of his blue and yellow tunic and very gingerly holding the mate to the gun in my own hand. He laid it gently on the ground then, slowly, and for some reason never taking his eyes from the gun in my hand, he started to ease away from me.

With my empty hand I waved him to come back and then pointed to his friend resting so comfortably, it looked to me, on the broad step.

His eyes never leaving me, he moved in, slipped his hands under his friend's armpits and, puffing more than seemed necessary, dragged him off, his heels trailing, and into a small black and white skimmer I now saw parked a short distance off.

Black and white. It's not too far away, but the light there is even poorer than it is here. It could be a dark ... no, stay with your first impression. You were right about the red. You're right this time, too. Black and white, it is.

Green. The taillights are green, but that's not fair because they light up from inside. No matter, they're out of sight now anyway.

Anton Plagiar's bully boys. What could they have wanted?

I became aware of a weight in my hand and forced my eyes to focus on it.

A handgun. What was a laser-beam handgun doing in my hand?

It felt sticky, and the red on it was all up and down the sleeve of my jumpsuit. And after the police had just gone to all that trouble to clean it for me, too.

I shrugged and looked around for a place to throw the gun. None seemed about to present itself, so I loosened my grip on the gun butt and let it fall right where I stood.

It landed with a clatter and a sound of solid

metal striking. Interesting, I thought. You'd expect to hear the solid sound first and then the clatter.

Or maybe that was the way it had been. The thud and then the clatter. Or was it the clatter and *then* the thud?

It was easy enough to find out, just drop the gun again and listen closely this time.

But to do that I'd have to stoop down to pick it up.

Stoop down.

I considered that and the gun at my feet for a long, long time. Then I shrugged. What was the difference if I couldn't keep a sequence of sounds straight. I was great on colors, wasn't I?

I turned and made my way into the transhaus through its slowly revolving doors. My head. Would the blasted humming in it never ease up?

Chapter Eleven

He was following me, I was sure of it now, and it made me nervous.

I had a right to be nervous.

The spattering of blood, dry and brown now, on my sleeve. I must have been out of my head to take on two of Plagiar's bully boys. Two, with guns, and me, with my bare hands and no brains.

I shook my head. It felt better now and, when I flexed my fingers, the phasing of their strength was more of an annoyance than an actual hazard.

But the man dogging me was making me nervous. I could have turned and walked up to him and asked him point-blank what he had in his mind. But how could I know what he had in those hands deep in his baggy pockets; and the way I was feeling about it right now, I'd just about used up all the luck any mortal was reasonably entitled to in my scuffle last night with Plagiar's men.

He was tall and fairly broad, and his hair was as white as Plagiar's, but he wore it cut short and standing straight up. And he had glasses. Thick, dark-rimmed, Earthside glasses.

Somehow, I had the feeling that he'd come out of the transhaus only shortly before I did.

I eased my record camera out of my sleeve pocket, cocked and aimed it over my shoulder backward and hidden in my palm.

I made the exposure and slipped the camera back into my sleeve pocket, noting the picture's number in the tiny tab window so that I could play it back for the transhaus clerk to look at if I got the chance.

The transhaus clerk. He was an antiseptic-looking youth I didn't remember having seen before.

"Where's the manager?" I'd asked him when I came up from my sleep cubicle and stopped in for my receipted sleep-bill, and to ask him about a place to eat.

"He is my uncle," the boy said. "We have not seen him these twenty-four hours and we are greatly concerned.

"Oh?" I said, and thanked him for the directions to a nearby gasthaus that served food at all hours.

"No thanks are necessary," he told me, and it began to dawn on me that this was the Poldrogi way of expressing a simple "You're welcome."

Almost as an afterthought, I turned back from the revolving door. "What's your uncle's name?" I asked the boy.

"Kval," he said. "Piot Kval."

Piot Kval. The manager of the transhaus where I slept, and I had told the police I didn't know the man.

The corporal was entitled to his skeptical look, it would appear. And I had no doubt at all that if Kval stayed missing much longer, the corporal would let his attitude of disbelief change to something more unpleasant for me than just an attitude.

Twenty-four hours. Poldrogi's very rapid day-and-night sequence made it confusing for an offworlder to keep track of time, but twenty-four hours ago...?

I checked off the hours in my head. Twenty-four would take it back to just about the time that Brigit had been in Kval's office and waiting for me.

But he was not there when I saw her, so I might very well have been the last person to talk to him when he'd come to awaken me and tell me of Brigit.

And my questioning by the police suddenly took on a nasty point.

Kval had been out of his office, but Brigit expected him back, else why did she leave the two double-eagles on his desk for him?

Or maybe she had good reason to know that he wouldn't be back and the double-eagles were a subterfuge ... to fool me.

Forty dollars worth of subterfuge? I shook my head. I fooled cheaper than that.

But she had seen him, he'd told me she had ... and if he turned up completely vanished or dead, I had a sinking feeling I knew who would be near the top of the police list of prime suspects.

And I also knew that escape from the planet was out of the question. I didn't have the money for standard passage ... and stowing away would let me stay aboard ship only until the first search-robot nosed past my would-be hiding place.

Brigit. I had to find out for the sake of my own neck what that near-lethal gambit at the Wayfarer's Home was all about.

Some killer had tried to make me a patsy ... and someone had nearly nailed me with a masher beam. A camera that should have been smashed was as perfect as when it was new.

And the bully boys. If the blood on my sleeve was any indication, I'd somehow managed to cut up one of them elsewhere than in just his pride ... and I had no hope that either of them was of the forgive-and-forget school of thought.

And I was hungry. Lord, was I hungry. Except for the hot drink at the police barracks that my phasing stomach refused to hold, I'd had no food since before meeting Brigit.

Brigit ... and Plagiar ... but first of all, food.

I let the slowly revolving door of the transhaus carry me through and it was then that I noticed the tall man with the straight-up hair and the heavy glasses begin to follow me.

Chapter Twelve

I flicked on the gasthaus table radio and listened to the newscast while I shoveled food into my mouth. When they came around to the weather prediction for the second time and still hadn't mentioned the brouhaha at the Wayfarer's Home, or that one of their citizens was missing, I turned it off.

But I did not stop eating and it was only when I was about two-thirds of the way through the second portion that the table-boy had brought me that I looked up from my work to eye the tall man at the far end of the room who was making a poor job of not looking at me through his heavy-rimmed glasses.

He'd taken more than a decent interval to come into the gasthaus after me, and he sat alone at his round table now, worrying the one large cup of local tea he'd picked up and getting very hard stares from his table-boy.

The food in my stomach was having its effect, and he didn't look quite so menacing. In fact, now that I was pointedly staring at him as I ate, I saw that he was beginning to fidget.

Or, if not actually fidget, then to twitch in his

seat like a man with something on his mind that he would rather not have there. A fish out of water, a man in over his depth.

My open staring must have added to the way he was feeling. He hunched around in his seat until his back was toward me, and I saw his head bobbing slightly up and down as though he were talking to somebody. Only the chair opposite him at his table was empty.

Then abruptly he shoved back his chair and his cup and got up in almost the same motion. He turned and came directly toward me with a deep scowl on his face.

He stopped so close that his small pot of a stomach was almost in my face. I don't like a pepper-and-salt pattern, and I like it even less up against my snout. His baggy jumpsuit had a musty smell to it, like something locked up and long forgotten.

"Sklar," he said in a voice that was almost belligerent. "I'm Dr. Rolf Sklar. May I sit down?"

He said the name as though it ought to mean something to me. It didn't. And I didn't like his stomach in my face.

Or maybe it was just that my belly was close to being full. "You can drop dead if you like, friend," I said and dropped my eyes back to my plate.

I'd dropped my eyes, but I'd seen the flicker of a pained look in his face, and I realized that his belligerence could very well be directed, not at me, but at himself. Here, indeed, was a fish out of its element.

I apologized for maybe misreading him but only in my head. Aloud I said nothing. I let him stand there while I went on eating.

He took a long time deciding, but when he did I heard him let out his breath in a gasping wheeze.

On the rim of my vision I saw him reach into an inside pocket of his baggy jumpsuit and come out with something that he laid on the table in front of me.

My eyes couldn't help flicking to it, but I had them back on my plate in an instant.

He sighed and opened the folded-over bit of heavy paper and flattened it out with short, twitching motions of his long, spadelike fingers.

Circles, I didn't quite make out the first digit, but the zeros that came after it impressed me. A sight-draft for five figures. Ten thousand Earth credits at the least and maybe more if I was willing to appear interested enough to look at the chit closely enough to be sure I was seeing it aright.

I didn't look.

The man who'd called himself Sklar and a doctor sighed again, this time with a quavering sound. "It's all I have," he said. "All I could get together. Tell me where the boy is."

I felt myself sweating, and it wasn't all the fault of Poldrogi's heat or the suddenly stuffy air of the gasthaus.

This was a man who thought I knew something ... and something valuable enough to lay out five figures worth of credits for. His all, if he was to be believed.

"You have got the wrong table," I said. "I don't know what you're talking about."

He pulled back the chair opposite and slammed himself down into it. "Look," he said, right into my face, "I'm not a devious man. This is all the cash

I have and it's all there is, and I might just be giving you a way out. Think about that."

Cheese. That local green cheese with the heavy streaks of white and blue mold running through it. He'd had cheese for breakfast.

"I still don't know what you're talking about," I said.

"I said I'm not a devious man and I'm not, but I was at the Wayfarer's House yesterday and I saw what happened."

He let his voice trail off and sat looking at me as though what he'd just said was supposed to have a special meaning for me.

It did, but it was not what he thought it should have, I was willing to bet.

It had started to occur to me that maybe that sniper's shot at me wasn't the lucky near-miss I'd taken it to be at all. That I had been set up as a patsy, but not for an assassination attempt. This could be the reverse play.

I'd been thinking that someone had wanted to kill Plagiar and then nail me before I could be arrested and given the chance to deny it.

It could very well be that the sniper didn't want Plagiar dead and had never intended to hit me. That the only intent behind the shot had been to make me look important enough to kill.

Important enough to kill and so important enough to contact and offer money to for information about a boy.

Important enough to be a red herring across somebody else's trail.

And it had worked, else why was this obviously agitated man sitting opposite me, leaning so close his cheesy breath was near to ruining my breakfast and peering at me through his thick glasses?

But where did a missing transhaus manager fit in ... if he fit in at all? And the green dye that had almost gotten me lynched by a mob? And Plagiar's bully boys ... must not forget Plagiar's bully boys.

I shook my head and Sklar misunderstood the motion. He snatched up his sight-draft and jammed it back into his inside pocket. "All right," he snapped. His obvious frustration made his voice almost a snarl. "Have it your way, then. I said that I'm not a devious man and I'm not. If you live long enough to change your mind, I'm staying at the Matruza."

He slammed back his chair and was stalking out of the gasthaus before that crack about living long enough to change my mind made its way past my ears and into my head.

I was still shaking my head when I looked up from staring into my plate and saw that I was about to have another visitor.

Bearing down on me, mouth all pulled down and dark eyes intense looking, was Brigit.

Brigit Plagiar ... and behind her were two bully boys and one of them had pale skin patches on his chin, his lip, and his nose; his right hand stiff with splints and bandages.

His eyes, boring hotly into mine as our glances met, were not friendly.

Chapter Thirteen

Anger? Fear? Anxiety? I tried to read the look on Brigit's face as she drew closer to me, the bully boys making a kind of counterpoint backdrop to divide my scrutiny.

Then, suddenly, her face was pleasant but disinterested; and the two bully boys were just a couple of stocky young men in blue and yellow tunics pulling back chairs and looking around for a table-boy.

Then it broke through to me, too, the double tone beeping sound of police vehicles coming to a stop out front.

I caught at Brigit's wrist as she came close and started to move on past me. She did not resist, did not try to pull away. She stood there, face pleasant, looking neither to the right nor to the left. When I caught on and released my hold, she went on to a table close by the kitchen door as if she'd never broken her stride since first she'd stepped into the gasthaus.

The police corporal. I recognized him even with his bald head hidden under a uniform cap. He stopped by my table but did not sit down. He seemed no friendlier than the last time I'd seen him, but then he seemed no more hostile either.

THE RIM-WORLD LEGACY AND BEYOND 75

"Mr. Pike," he said. "I would like to speak with you."

"Sit down," I said, pushing the leftovers on my plate around with some pretense of not being finished with my breakfast.

"Elsewhere," he said.

"Am I under arrest?" I asked.

There was only the briefest of pauses before the corporal said, "May I see your identification, please."

My identification card was in my card case. So was my CE license.

I pushed back my chair and stood up. "I read you," I said. "Loud and clear."

The corporal did not flicker an eyelid. "This way, please," he said, and I followed him outside the gasthaus.

Three police skimmers? Just to pick up one ex-SpaceNav Photo Mate? It didn't seem possible.

It wasn't.

"A moment, please," the corporal said, and walked to the last skimmer in the line to lean inside it.

When he came back, he was draping a small shiny gray plastic box on a lanyard around his neck. He slid the tiny black control button on its side down to the lock position and the square window that was a kind of lid to the box glowed amber.

A signal damper.

It gave off no sound the human ear could hear, and would not interfere with airborne vibration so that it did not hamper normal speech. But any electronic pickup within the small sphere of its silent signal would deliver back at its home end nothing more than a crackling, undecipherable hiss.

I looked around. Who did he think would be listening in on us out here?

But the corporal was speaking to me. "Come," he said, "it is not far."

It wasn't. Only the retracing of the brief distance I'd come from the transhaus.

Nothing could be handier to a spaceport than its transhaus accommodations. Accommodations whose skeleton went in even before the substructure of the field itself was laid down. You had to house your workers somewhere, and it was easier and less wasteful of expensive building materials to dig a hole than to put up comparably-sized aboveground facilities.

And after your construction crews debarked for other planets and other jobs, they left behind ready-made housing that, while not fancy, could not have been any handier.

The transhaus clerk, when I'd spoken to him earlier, had seemed young to be substituting for his uncle. Now, sitting against the wall with a police private in the chair behind the desk, he looked barely into his teens. And when he led us down the ramp to the first level below the field surface, his head, seen from behind, seemed to wiggle and dip as though it were too large and too heavy for its shaved neck to carry. He was blond, as I suppose his bald uncle might once have been.

We came to the end of the corridor and the boy slid open a panel marked with a scrubbed and faded "B." He stepped back, his face turned away.

The corporal motioned me forward. The boy's uncle, the fat manager, pressed into a corner, the meaty shoulders kept upright by the angle of the walls, the arms and legs sprawling.

A stain, small, almost lost in the larger, faded ones on the T-shirt that had the color of dry and faded blood.

A stain, small and under the heart. A laser wound that bled little since its killer beam, searing as it pierced, locked in all but the ooze.

"How long?" I asked, but I knew the answer.

"He's been dead some thirty-six hours, give or take a few," the corporal said. "We will pin it down later. The boy found him when he came down for a refill cylinder for their disinfecting system."

And now I noticed that the room was small and obviously used for the storage of dull, squat, gas cylinder shapes.

I saw the corporal eyeing the blood spatters on the sleeve of my jumpsuit. "Do you still deny knowing him?" he asked.

I pulled my sleeve around. "This isn't his blood," I protested. "I didn't have it when he was killed. You know that. You cleaned this suit yourself."

"I asked if you still deny knowing him?"

"No, I don't deny it. I wouldn't have denied it yesterday if you'd told me who he was. I only found out his name an hour ago."

The corporal shrugged. "Yesterday I was asking about a man who'd been gone only a matter of hours. A small favor for an employer who was concerned about a man missing from the job he should have been filling. An employer who would have thought it no favor if by seeming to press with my questions I should give rise to rumors. A missing manager, even if no funds are gone with him . . . a statement many would have their own ideas about

... cannot help but reflect on the rest of a man's establishment."

"This," I said, pointing at the dead man, "this is going to help his business?"

"Ah," said the corporal. "This we must assume his employer did not know about."

The boy who had guided us to the storeroom stood, his back to us, ramrod straight. The corporal touched his shoulder. "All right, Fraan," he said. "You can go back to work now."

The boy left without so much as looking back.

"They lived alone," the corporal said, his voice unexpectedly sympathetic. "Perhaps now that his uncle is gone, he will go back to his home world." He shook his head and in the same sympathetic tone of voice said to me, "What did the doctor want for his twenty thousand credits?"

"He said . . ." and then I caught myself. "I didn't know what he was talking about," I said. I might not tell the corporal all I could remember of what Dr. Rolf Sklar had said to me, but he was no man I wanted to start lying to either.

Twenty thousand? Twenty thousand credits? I had purposely kept my eyes averted from Sklar's sight-draft, but I thought he'd said ten thousand. I played the sound of his voice back in my head . . . yes, he had said ten thousand was all he had. My instinct had been right, so much for the edgy doctor's believability.

Aloud I said, "how did you know he offered me anything at all?"

The corporal did not answer my question. He said, "I make no threats, Mr. Pike. I merely point out that you were here when Piot was killed . . . or at least the time sheet upstairs would indicate that he made no entry to check you out when you left...."

Time sheet. Transhaus sleep cubicles. You paid for them in advance and by the hour as you used them. If you had time between starships and wanted to spend it resting up after the bout of warp-sickness you'd just been through, you checked into a transhaus.

And, because the time needs varied so greatly, there never were, and never had been any arbitrary day minimums, or even noon to midnight charges. If you stayed an hour, you paid for an hour. If you were a photographer who had reason to watch his credits, you checked in to sleep ... and you checked out ... and when you did, you had to do it with the manager to make sure that you hadn't overstayed your declared and paid for time.

Piot Kval hadn't checked me out; might even have been dead when I followed Brigit out of his office.

Brigit ... and the forty dollars she'd left for a dead man.

I became aware of the silence and realized that the corporal was waiting for me to answer the question he'd just put to me.

Fingerprints ... it was something about fingerprints.... Did I deny that the print on the safebox lockplate was mine? Was it, perhaps, a clever forgery?

I shook my head. No, I did not deny that. Early in their use, it had been discovered that the lockplate, which electronically scrutinized the pattern of ridges and whorls on the thumb presented to it when its lid was closed, could be opened by simply presenting the same pattern in the shape of a print lifted from a water glass ... or even a one-to-one photograph. Redesigning of the device was immediate, and now the record included a reading of the electrical potential of the skin that formed the ridges so that the thumb presented had at least to be alive. Still, boxes were being opened, and the tug-of-war between designer and thief was a continuing one.

"Thirty-six hours ago I was here," I said to the corporal. "I was here and I spoke to the manager. He called me to an assignment and the last I saw of him he was walking away from me. Back to his office for all I know."

"Ah, yes, the assignment. The affair at the Wayfarer's Home."

"Yes," I said, and I wondered if I ought to tell him to verify my story with Brigit, that she, too, had been here.

But if she'd had anything to do with Kval's death, she'd hardly own up to it, and her denial would just make any statement of mine that much less plausible and me that much more suspect.

Suspect. So far the corporal hadn't made any specific accusation, just seemed bent on making me out a liar.

"And the twenty thousand credits ... what was that for?"

It was the second time he'd asked that question. "I've already told you," I said. "I have no idea what Sklar was talking about ... I didn't even know his name until he told me what it was ... and I still don't know who he is."

I must have sounded on a short leash because the corporal held up a pudgy hand. "I do not mean to try your patience, Mr. Pike, but let us consider.

"You are a photographer, not well known and of . . ." he looked about him at the scrubbed and faded transhaus walls, ". . . of less than affluent means. Yet you are singled out to photograph a man of no small prominence . . . a distinguished visitor.

"You are bedaubed by a dye we use only for riots . . . yet none of my men has done this to you. They, in fact, must rescue you from a mob pursuing you for reasons none can now explain except in the vaguest of terms. They thought you a menace to their children . . . and no one can remember who first raised the cry against you.

"You have told me that you were fired upon by a sniper and there is evidence that some weapon was indeed used. But it is not evidence of a masher beam, Mr. Pike. It is evidence of a cutting laser . . . and from its angle it came from no distant point, but rather from the platform itself. The platform, Mr. Pike, that you were on."

I started to protest, but the corporal showed me his palm again.

"Furthermore, a citizen on his way to work finds two pistols and spatters of blood on the step of your transhaus, and its manager is found dead in a storeroom, killed, it would appear, at a time that you have just admitted to being on his premises."

He pointed at my sleeve. "You have blood on a sleeve that we both know was clean less than twelve hours ago.

"A man is seen outside a bank apparently waiting for it to open so that he can transfer all his funds into a draft account and shortly afterward this same man is heard offering it all to you for information you tell him, and now me, that you do not have."

Heard? Sklar was heard talking to me? He hadn't particularly kept his voice down, but there simply hadn't been time for anyone to have passed the information on to the corporal ... or to anyone at all. Sklar had left, and the police had come upon the scene almost at once ... and no one had made a hurried exit that I'd seen.

The corporal was still pegging his points at me. "The doctor did not seem to believe your plea of ignorance was genuine. He gave you his address at the Matruza should you change your mind."

I goggled at the corporal. He had the words exactly.

He went on coldly, but almost ruefully. "For a man who claims innocence and ignorance, you have been subjected to a singular series of happenings."

And then his voice went unmistakably flat. "All right, Pike, do you want to tell me what is really going on? A falling out among thieves? Did your partner get greedy, Pike? Or did he get scared when he found out how big a man your intended victim is ... and it was silence him or drop the whole enterprise?

"But that isn't the most unfortunate part is it, Pike? The most unfortunate part is now that the whole affair has curdled, you are still as lacking of funds as you ever were ... and it must be galling to you that you cannot accept any that might fall your way for fear of breaking the mask of innocence ... of ignorance, you have chosen to wear. Tell me, Pike, what does Sklar want for his twenty thousand?"

"I don't know!" I shouted, and I didn't know if what I was feeling was anger or dismay at the incredibility of my predicament. "I don't know. I don't know what he was talking about. I don't know who killed Kval. I don't know what is going on. I don't know!"

The corporal laughed, a nasty sound. "Have it your way," he said. "There are others in this with you and I frankly expect you to deny all ... but I will not take you with me. I want only for the moment to give to the others a sense of urgency when they think of you."

I could feel the scar on the top of my head begin to prickle. "What ... what are you driving at?" I said to the corporal.

"Always the pretense of ignorance, is it not so, Mr. Pike? Very well, I will enlighten you. You do not, then, know of the transmitter in your wrist-chrono?"

I stared at the tiny timepiece on my wrist, "A transmitter? In my wrist-chrono?"

"In the stem, to be exact. Our laboratory discovered it when they went over your clothes while you were our guest."

I stared at him, gaped is a better word. "A transmitter...? But who...?

He chuckled, another unpleasant sound. "It is an interesting question for you to ponder. Who, indeed? It is a tiny unit and its scrambler not a particularly sophisticated one. We were able to break its pattern with very little trouble. I heard you speaking to the doctor, Mr. Pike, but who else also did?"

He fingered the gray shape of the signal damper glowing on the lanyard around his neck. "What I say to you now, have said to you since we were together, has not been heard by anyone, of course, and it has perhaps set them to wondering. It is my hope that it is so."

He smiled at me, showing me hand-carved teeth like those of the dead Kval. "You see, Mr. Pike, I am setting you up as a ..." he groped for the word, "... decoy? No, that is not the word ... one of those things that is shot at ... a duck ... a sitting duck. Yes, Mr. Pike, I am setting you out as a sitting duck to be shot at in the hope that the hunter will by this act betray himself."

Decoy ... duck ... he was splitting hairs. I stared, fascinated, at the timepiece on my wrist.

"It does present you with something of a problem, doesn't it, Mr. Pike. Should you leave your transmitter where it is and have your every word, the very sound of your breathing listened to by whom? Where? Or should you tear it out and cut the betraying link? But if you do that, Mr. Pike, you will also break your tie with me. Your listener will not be able to hear you, but then neither will I should he drive you into a corner from which there is no escape."

The corporal seemed to be genuinely enjoying himself. "You have an interesting decision to make, Mr. Pike. An interesting decision."

He put a thumb on the tiny black control button of his signal damper. "And now, Mr. Pike, the best of luck," and he slid the button up and into the "off" position.

The amber light behind its small window went out and I knew that my every movement, my every mutter would carry and be heard—where? By whom?

The corporal touched a finger to the peak of his uniform cap and walked away from me toward the end of the corridor. Just before he went out of my sight he turned, showed me his teeth again.

"Quack, quack," he said and his cold chuckle as he went up the ramp was loud enough to carry back to me.

To me, standing, staring at the stem of my wristchrono, rubbing unabashedly at the scar on my head.

Who? Where? And just when had he ... they ... she had the chance to plant it to begin with? How long had I been carrying it? Hours ago? Or planets ago?

How long has someone had his finger on me?

Chapter Fourteen

Anton Plagiar raised an eyebrow at me. "My wife? When did you ever meet my wife?" His tone was ordinary enough, but again I sensed the latent power of the man.

I glanced uncertainly around the sitting room of his hostel suite, at the two bully boys standing easy at the anteroom door, the new skin patches on the face of the taller one very prominent to my eyes at the moment; the fingers of his hand, stiff in their splints and bandages, inescapable.

"I . . . she hired me. She hired me to take pictures of you during your magic act."

He laughed, it was a short laugh and not one that sounded amused at all. "I haven't seen my wife for months, and I can assure you that the last thing she would want is a picture of me and what it pleases her to call my childish carrying on."

"But," I said, and I wondered what kind of a trap it was that I had managed to walk myself into. My wrist-chrono that held a direct line to the listener, but also to the corporal if I got into a bind, was carefully locked in the safebox at the foot of my transhaus bunk.

I'd had a feeling of satisfaction that bordered on the smug when that gambit dawned on me. The corporal thought he'd left me with the hard choice of leaving the transmitter where it was and risking betrayal through the sounds that I made or what might be said to me, or tearing it out and so warning my unknown listener that I knew of him and thus perhaps bringing him down on me from a quarter I could not begin to suspect.

What was simpler, though, than to leave the transmitter untouched but to deceive the ears that listened?

Brigit. Brigit had seemed to me to be the one with answers I needed desperately to know, so I waited until it was believably late enough, faked the sounds of turning in and then, leaving my timepiece behind, I had come as unobtrusively as I could to the hostel at which I'd expected to find her.

I hadn't hoped that I could avoid Plagiar and speak to Brigit alone, but neither had I expected him to laugh at the prospect of my having met his wife.

He laughed again. This time he sounded amused, and I was sure I heard a snicker from the bully boys by the door. Plagiar motioned with his hand, pointing at an inner door of his suite, and one of his bully boys vanished through it.

The man was back in a moment and the woman with him was Brigit.

"Brigit," Plagiar said, "did you hire this man to take pictures of me?"

Brigit settled herself in a corner of one of the room's several sofas. "Yes and no," she said. "I thought it might be well to have him where we could see him when I heard that Sklar had been recognized."

I hadn't heard Plagiar say anything to her about his wife, so I knew she'd been listening from the other room when she added, "I knew he couldn't refuse if I told him I was your wife."

Refuse? She hadn't given me a chance to. We were in her skimmer and on our way before she told me who she was.

Plagiar smiled, but at the same time he shook his head. "Some day, Brigit, your little habit of not bothering me with details is going to make me very unhappy with you."

He turned his attention to me. "Sklar offered you twenty thousand. I'll double his figure. Where is the boy?"

I shook my head. I wasn't answering him, I was just trying to clear it. First the corporal, and now both Brigit and Plagiar; all were taking for granted or trying to force a relationship between me and a man I had never seen, never even heard of until scant hours ago.

Twenty thousand. The same figure that the corporal had used, yet I was sure that it was a wrong one. Could Plagiar have it from the same source as the corporal? Was he the listener?

If he was, he should have shown some sign of surprise at seeing a man he thought to be in his bunk and asleep walk into the room. I hadn't seen any such reaction, but then would a man get to be as powerful as he if he had a face that showed anything but what he wanted it to show?

My head wasn't clear and I hadn't stopped shaking it. Plagiar made a small gesture of impatience.

"All right. Fifty thousand, but I warn you, Pike, I intend to have the boy."

Protesting that I had no idea what they were talking about had gotten me exactly nowhere with anyone, but I had to give it a go.

"I don't know what you're talking about," I said to Plagiar, and my luck with the flat statement was no better than before.

He nodded. "A very sensible attitude for you to take, but you will understand if I find it hard to accept that it was sheer coincidence that brought you to Kval's establishment . . . or that it was a case of mistaken identity that led someone to try for you with a masher beam.

"I might add that for a moment my men mistook your firing back with your camera gun as an attempt on me, until they saw that you were fighting to keep it pointed downward."

He smiled and looked at his bully boys before he came back to me. "I'm sorry about the dye," he said. "But a police weapon that does not kill often avoids a serious probing, yet it can be remarkably effective."

All right. So the bully boys fired at me by mistake. But who raised the cry afterward that sent the mob after me? Or was that a mistake, too? Hardly.

I had the feeling of pressures within pressures, of attacks within attacks . . . and who had cleaned up my camera for the police?

But Plagiar was answering that. "A weapon in your camera," he was saying, "how venerable a device. But I do not mean to criticize. I took the liberty of having it removed for fear that if the police found it they might jump to a completely unwarranted conclusion that could only cause misunderstanding and embarrassment all around."

So you don't want the police nosing about, but if you took the laser out, then you know it didn't simply jam.

"Thank you," I said, and there was complete silence while we all stared at each other.

I broke it with the first thing that came into my mind. "Kval is dead," I said.

"Yes," Plagiar nodded. "Frankly, I did not recognize him, he'd grown so fat ... and what a name to assume: Kval, *Smith*. It is enough to arouse suspicion on any planet. But that he should be killed did surprise me ... until I learned of you."

We were back to me again ... and now, in their minds, I was tied to a man who'd had reason to hide his once thin body under layers of fat ... and his real name behind the dirt common one of Smith, Kval.

And he was dead.

I'd come looking for Brigit and for some answers. I'd also come because, remembering the bully boys and why they'd accosted me on the transhaus step, I'd half reasoned it might go easier to confront Plagiar before he issued a second invitation.

So now I knew who'd cleaned up my camera but not who planted the laser.

I knew that if Plagiar hadn't heard of me until after Kval was dead then he hadn't planted the transmitter ... and he wasn't the listener.

I didn't know who had ... and I didn't know when. Least of all did I know why.

The boy, Plagiar'd called his quarry. There was a boy worth fifty thousand to him. Fifty thousand!

Who was he? Why was everyone so positive I knew where he was?

And Kval, who might have known, was dead.

Plagiar was looking at me ... Brigit was looking at me. I turned. The two bully boys by the door were looking at me.

I made a move toward the door, but neither of the bully boys looked as though he had any mind to step aside for me.

I turned back to Plagiar. I tried not to think that I'd cleverly put my line to the corporal out myself when I'd left the transmitter off my wrist ... that I'd taken some small pains to leave the transhaus without being seen. Who knew I was in Plagiar's suite? Had ever been, if I turned up missing.

I cleared my throat. I had a bargaining point, but it had validity only as long as Plagiar believed what I knew was not so. That I knew the whereabouts, if not the identity, of some as yet unnamed "boy."

And it was dawning on me that, valid or not, it was the only bargaining point I did have.

"I'll think about it," I said to Plagiar, and knew as I said the words that by them I affirmed as true something I knew was not. "Fifty thousand is a lot of money."

Plagiar did not move and neither did his bully boys, and the conditioned air of Poldrogi indoors was suddenly more than chilling to me.

He spoke, and it seemed to me completely off the subject.

"Pike," he said, "how did you find me?"

I hadn't, but I said, "You're a big man, all I had to do was ask."

"Remember that when you think, Pike. Remember that fifty thousand is a lot of money ... and that I'm a big man."

I nodded. I did not trust myself to speak.

The bully boys stepped aside and I was almost at the doorway when Plagiar called my name.

The bully boys snapped back together to block my path at once.

"It has just struck me," Plagiar said, "that I might be misinterpreting your interest in Kval . . . or his in you. This will take but a moment, and it will ease my mind about you. You will indulge me?"

He'd put it as a question, but I knew an order when I heard one.

I didn't say anything, I didn't nod, I just stood there.

At Plagiar's nod, Brigit and a bully boy left the room and when they came back he was pushing what looked like an oversize magician's taboret on wheels.

From the way it moved, it was heavy. Too extravagant of weight to be anything but a major illusion.

I searched Brigit's face for some inkling of what Plagiar had in mind, but she did not lift her eyes from the rolling tabletop in front of her.

The unit was upright and about the size of a large trunk standing on end. Its broad top was unmarred except for a slit some two inches long, and a yellow-metal disk about the size of a double-eagle coin, set about an inch below the surface.

"Touch it," Plagiar said.

I looked at him, not understanding.

"Touch it," he repeated, pointing to the disk.

I touched it.

I felt a rubbing sensation, as though an invisible edge in the disk had scraped across the flesh of my finger as I pressed against it.

A pause. Long enough for me to feel the blood

pound twice in my ears, and then a tiny ding and a card shot up out of the slit to quiver on the end of a slender rod that held it a foot or so above the tabletop.

It was a trey. The trey of diamonds.

All this equipment to produce a single card?

But Plagiar hadn't looked at it. "Thank you," he said. "I knew it was impossible, yet there are always rumors. It was easy enough to check. Thank you again."

He seemed relaxed now, cordial even.

I wasn't.

For some reason, the touching of the taboret and the wait had pulled me up tight enough to twang. And Plagiar's easy manner didn't soothe me any.

Nor did it help me to have the taller bully boy, the one with the patches on the parts of his face I'd clipped with his own gun, lean into me with his shoulder as I went past him.

He did not send me sprawling. I don't think he meant to. He just shoved, and I got his point.

The point and the sound of Plagiar's laughter followed me through the anteroom and out into the corridor.

Stepping out of the hostel's slowly revolving main door I got another jolt.

Across the night-deserted street and far up it; too far for me to be sure of what I saw even in the glare of the crime-lights, I sensed a sudden movement. A tall, broad, white-haired figure stepping back or darting out of sight, or maybe the rim of my vision had caught him in a momentary peering forth from a hiding place.

Rolf Sklar? I couldn't be sure.

I scanned the entire street. Not a sign of motion.

No tall figure, no black and white police skimmers, not a single pair of privates in sweaty brown uniforms patrolling their beat.
I saw nobody.
Nobody.
I was alone.

Chapter Fifteen

Rocks.

I had to have a more than sizable assortment of them in my head to be standing here in the dark at the side of the raw country road, waiting for the one person to show up who'd sucked me into this imbroglio to begin with.

Brigit.

The bully boy with the patches on his face had shoved me, hard, as I passed him on my way out of Plagiar's suite. I took it to be a natural resentment for the favor I'd done his looks with his own gun. I was down in the street before I thrust my hands deep into my jumpsuit pockets and felt the tiny stiffness in one of them.

I stopped under the nearest crime-light to read the note. On a scrap of paper that looked like a corner torn from a larger sheet, the message was classic.

"I must see you. The road behind the Wayfarer's Home. In an hour."

I looked at the signature again to be sure I wasn't reading it wrong. A firm hand, small, initial caps large, the crossbar on the T a dagger slash. *Brigit*.

In an hour, in the dark, and thrust into my pocket by the bully boy who owed me no favors for the patches on his face.

Great.

The word taxi was unknown beyond the limits of the town and the spaceport, so I'd ridden as far as I could and walked the rest of the way. It could have taken me an hour. I didn't know, my timepiece was still sending its signal from inside the safebox at the transhaus.

Rolf Sklar, whoever he was, seemed sure, at least ten thousand credits worth, that I knew something that I didn't know. Maybe twenty thousand.

About the police corporal I could have no doubt. He was convinced I knew something I didn't know.

And Plagiar. Plagiar hadn't said the words, but he was giving me only the shortest of possible times to make up my mind to tell him what he wanted to know ... and what I didn't know.

I sighed. All I needed now was for Brigit to hit me with the same line, when she showed up.

If she showed up.

She showed up.

And I got it.

It was dark, but all the same I stared in the direction of her voice.

"You can't mean it," I said. "If anybody should know that I don't even know what they're talking about, it should be you. You picked me out of the air to begin with."

In Poldrogi's moonless blackness, I could make out no more than the simple feeling of her presence, but the shrug was plain enough in her off-world accented voice.

"I did not exactly pick you out of the air, as you

say. Your name and your ..." she fumbled for a word, "... your place of staying were given me."

She had come looking for me, armed with my name and location? But who could know I was on Poldrogi, who could even care? It was a big galaxy; surely there had to be another Pike, even one named Eli who was a photographer. She had to be mistaken.

I told Brigit so.

She did not contradict me, but from her voice it was plain that she did not believe me. It was also plain that here was a woman who thought she'd snagged a fish, thrown it back, and then discovered that what she'd taken to be a minnow was in reality a fat catfish.

A fat catfish.

Me.

I needed no great powers of perception to figure out she meant to get her hook back into me and her way was one that had worked for centuries ... and would keep on working for centuries to come.

But not tonight.

Not with me.

No matter how warm the dark night, no matter how heady the lure of her scent and the feel of her against me.

I had other things to think about and I didn't need the scar on the top of my head to keep them in mind. Lord, it was itching. And for once I was going to pay attention to it. I disentangled her arms from around me ... at least I went through the motions.

"There is money," she was saying against my chest. "More money than you or I can imagine ...

can ever dream about. There is power . . . there is everything . . . everything. . . ."

When I spoke, I spoke into her hair. "Why me?" I said. "Why did you come to me?"

Her shrug was a sinuous movement against me. "It was as I said to Anton. It was best that you be where we could see you, except . . ."

"Except what?"

"Except that I did not know when he told me where to find you that Sklar meant for you to die."

Die? Sklar? The masher beam? The ravenous mob?

"You must believe me. You must."

And if her arms around me could have matched in their strength the sincerity of her voice, I would have had bruises.

"You must believe I did not know he meant for you to die. I tried to warn you when I saw. You must remember that."

I remembered. I remembered her waving on the rim of my vision just as I pressed my camera release and the masher beam whirred past my head.

I remembered her waving, but I'd have to take her word for it that she meant it to be a warning.

"Sklar gave you my name . . . and tried to kill me? So why did he offer me all that money in the gasthaus? Try to shut me up and then offer me all his cash to talk?"

"He did not know that Kval was dead, and afterward . . . afterward there was only you to go to."

If Sklar did not know that Kval was dead when he took his shot at me, then it could not have been he who killed the transhaus manager. But if Brigit was lying and it hadn't been Sklar sniping, then he could be the killer.

In that case, who'd taken the shot at me . . . and why kill one of the only two men whom you think have information worth . . . what was it Brigit said? Money . . . power . . . everything?"

Or with two possible sources in mind, maybe whoever'd put the question to Kval hadn't felt a need to be overly careful with him. That left, if the killer thought like Brigit, only me.

Me . . . to keep alive . . . and she was trying her damnedest to weasel the information out of me.

"Tell me," she was repeating over and over . . . in different ways, but it all added up to the same thing. "Tell me where you have hidden the boy and I will go on from there. You will see. Trust me."

I'll bet you would, baby . . . and trust? Not hardly.

"Who is the boy?" I asked.

I felt her pull back, perhaps in surprise. "You do not know?"

From what she'd said it would appear that Kval and I were in this together. I took the chance.

"Kval did not tell me," I said. "Why would he?"

I could sense her chewing on that one.

"It is possible," she finally said, and from her voice, she was talking to herself more than to me. Then I felt the sudden tensing of her body ease and she was close to me again. Her hair brushing my chin and my lips as she nodded.

"Yes, I can see it was not only possible, but necessary. Kval would have been a fool to tell his accomplice the value of the boy. It is too much . . . too much to tempt a man with. It was best for him that he lead you to think it was no more than an ordinary act to work with him."

"You will tell me?" I asked, and I held my breath.

"Yes," she said. "After you take me to where he is."

I let out my breath. If I was standing up well to her personal brand of temptation, she wasn't about to try me with another kind.

I laughed. "Can you be sure I will lead you to the right boy? Do you know him?"

"Sklar knows him, of course, and Anton has his birth records, childhood pictures, things of that sort ... and the fingerprints from his school records ... and then there is the one sure test. You saw that."

"Yes," I said. "That one sure test."

The one sure test? I saw it?

There was a silence between us and I think both of us knew that we'd gone about as far in our exchange as each of us was going to get the other to go.

Brigit may not have gotten all that she'd arranged the meeting for, but she was sure, I felt, that she'd made her impression on me and that all I needed was a little time to work up a hankering.

And I'd added to my store of things to keep me worried.

"Another time," she said in my ear, and she may have brushed her lips against my cheek in the dark, I couldn't tell from the feel of it. It could just as easily have been the touch of a spider tendril trailing on the air or a night thing passing.

She was gone, back along the road from the sound of it. I heard her stumble and give a small gasp, and then the roar of her skimmer stoking up and taking off in the direction of the town.

I shrugged. I might have asked her for a lift to at least the edge of the transportation area if I'd thought of it ... if she hadn't left so quickly.

I settled myself for the long walk ahead of me.

I needn't have.

I walked only a few steps in the blackness and I found what it was that had made Brigit stumble, made her gasp.

I stumbled over it, too.

I fumbled in my sleeve pocket for my record camera. Its flash unit was the only light I had with me, but the split-second bursts would serve well enough.

I knew *what* I'd stumbled over.

I needed to know *who*.

Chapter Sixteen

It was hot. Stifling hot even for Poldrogi, and the police corporal's tunic was soaked with his sweat. On his desk stood his hand-fan, its blades unmoving. "Power," he'd said conversationally, when his men had brought me in. "Power, it is always a problem. I have used up its power pack and can get no other for I do not know how long. Power and weight, Mr. Pike. Power and weight, they are the problems we of the less favored worlds must cope with."

But he had long since stopped being conversational. "Would it surprise you," he was saying, "if I told you that your fingerprints were on the stone?"

"It sure would surprise me," I said. "I didn't know that a rock could take a print.

"There was blood on this one," he said.

"Blood or no blood, I did not touch the rock . . . or the body . . . or anything else. I just walked to the Wayfarer's Home and phoned you from there. How many times do you want me to repeat it?"

"And you photographed the body."

"Yes, I photographed the body, but I've already told you why."

"Of course. You wanted to see who it was."

"That's it. I needed my camera's lights to see by."

"And the other picture of the dead man we found when we played back your record. The one of him walking. Was the taking of it also prompted by curiosity?"

The shot of Rolf Sklar following me, the one I'd intended to show the transhaus clerk and never had.

"Yes," I said. "I wanted to know who he was."

"And now you know."

I let that one go. I was tired with the heat and the round-and-round sparring with the corporal. I had an unsettling feeling that a great deal of what I was gleaning from his questions were no slips of his lip. In the back of my head I kept hearing his "quack, quack."

Dr. Rolf Sklar. The "Dr." was honorary. An associate in philosophy at one of the lesser colleges. A place whose name I'd never heard before. That much came from his I.D. card.

The rest, what he was doing on Poldrogi and, more to the point, what he was doing on the road where I'd found him was up in the air.

Sklar, a crumpled heap in the brilliant split-second glare of my flashgun, fallen as though he'd already been in a half crouch when he was struck down.

But no woundless masher beam had slain him, no searing laser. Just a rock, large and heavy, smashed into the back of his skull and then let fall from the killer's hand.

And there was one item that had been separated from the small pile of his personal effects on the desktop in front of the corporal.

A small red container, thin, no larger than a postage stamp.

The corporal had slipped back its lid and pushed it forward for me to look at.

Tiny spindles, almost microscopic in size, each with a pill-shaped swelling at one end, each nested in its fitted pocket of soft foam.

Nine or ten in all, at least two of the pockets empty.

"What are they?" I said, feeling the cushioning softness of the foam with my fingertip.

"You have one in your timepiece," the corporal said. "Transmitters, identical with the one we found in your wrist-chrono."

Without thinking, my eyes flicked to the rest of Sklar's things in front of the corporal. I was looking for a radio, an earpiece, anything that might look as though it could pick up a signal.

"His glasses," I said, remembering their heavy rims, the temple pieces. "Did he have a receiver in his glasses?"

The corporal shook his head. "No," he said. "And that leaves you to wonder still who it is that is listening to you."

He looked pointedly at my empty wrist. "And he must soon begin to wonder how much sleep you take of a standard day."

Pretty much the same thought had been nagging at me. I put the box of transmitters back on the corporal's desk. "Are you holding me?" I asked.

He spread his hands. "What for? You found the body of a visitor who died, it would appear, violently. You reported it at once. This was most commendable, particularly since it was necessary for you to brave entering an area that had been less than hospitable to you on your previous visit."

Less than hospitable. The Wayfarer's Home was

the only place anywhere near to me that might have a line into the city when I stumbled over Sklar's body. And doors-with-no-inside-knobs or no, I had a more than public-spirited-citizen urge to keep my nose as clean as I possibly could.

It had occurred to me, not too many microseconds after the flicker of my camera's flashlamps had identified the body at my feet, to wonder if Brigit's gasp, which I'd heard when she stumbled upon the body, had been caused by that simple finding?

Or...?

Or had Sklar come with her to what they'd planned to make a trysting place in which she would entice me to give her the information they both seemed to want so badly?

Give it to her and then my usefulness over, my shield not only vanished, but my existence knowing what they thought I knew, a menace to them, was it *Sklar* who was to come up behind *me* with a rock?

And if it was, who had pounced soundlessly on him?

And what cover story was Brigit rushing to spread to make her own slim claim to innocence believable?

The Wayfarer's Home, a potential trap once I was inside it, had suddenly taken on the look of a haven.

The corporal was talking. "... and you have been very patient also with me and my poor, bumbling questions. I thank you."

Poor, bumbling questions.

It was a laugh, but I answered him in the local idiom. "No thanks are necessary."

He darted a sharp glance at me, and I learned the final reply in the Poldrogi ritual of thanks.

"True," he said. "True."

I turned to go, but he had one more thing to say to me. "Kval, if you do not already know, was not the other one's name."

The other one. A man is killed and for the living who must find his killer he is no longer an entity, a person. He is a body, a thing, *the other one.*

"I had heard," I said, remembering Plagiar's amusement that the transhaus manager should have chosen so obvious a name behind which to hide. Kval. *Smith.*

"His papers were not authentic, they could not be, but our laboratory was able to detect no difference between them and our own issue. He, or whoever provided him with them, was a forger of an ability I have never before encountered. Baas, his name was, Mahar Baas."

And the corporal waited, his cold eyes under their sweat-beaded brows intent on me.

I gave no reaction. What reaction was there for me to give? Mahar Baas was as unknown a name to me as had been the one of Piot Kval.

"Where was he from?" I asked.

"Ah," said the corporal. "That is of interest. It would appear that he dropped out of sight some time ago, and with him some equipment about which the university people seem reluctant to be specific. At any rate, before he disappeared, Mahar Baas was some sort of laboratory assistant at. . . ."

And he named the planet and the college from which had come the murdered Dr. Rolf Sklar.

Chapter Seventeen

Brigit?

Or the boy?

I stood on the broad step of the police barracks, my mind racing.

It is one thing to meet a woman in the dark. It is another to meet her and to know that she, perhaps, means for you to be dead.

But the boy.

Sklar *knew* the boy.

Sklar is dead.

Sklar and Kval ... Baas. Both from the same planet, the same institution. Baas trying to hide.

Sklar and the transmitters? Nothing.

Hold ... Baas and the transmitters ... a memory stirring.

A memory of an acrid chemical bite in my nose and throat and of the pounding needed on the panels beside my head to bring me out of a deep sleep.

Before he'd awakened me to tell me of Brigit's presence in his office topside, had Baas cracked a sleep-gas capsule not too close to my face and taken advantage of the few moments so light an exposure would keep me deep asleep to reach into the wall pocket behind my head for my timepiece?

But why plant a transmitter on *me*? Had he recognized Brigit, but she not him? Or did each know fully who the other was, and did Baas have an end of his own in mind? A potential double cross?

Or was he acting under instructions from Brigit? Or from Sklar?

I shook my head. I seemed to be doing a lot of it. Plagiar.

Anton Plagiar. Brigit says he has the boy's school records, fingerprints, photographs.

He also knew Kval was not Kval but Baas. Knew it before Baas was dead.

Or did he?

He'd said that he didn't know Baas at first under all that fat. But had he seen him so *before* he was dead ... or *after*?

If *before*, then he could not help but know of the boy with him. Fraan, the transhaus clerk nephew.

But *Sklar* had known and still *he'd* come after me with his offer of money for a boy's whereabouts.

It followed, then, that Fraan was not the boy Plagiar or Sklar were after.

But Baas had tried to hide his identity behind a false name and under layers of body fat. Could he not have done the same for the boy?

Hormones, perhaps, to hold back a child's growth or to speed it up. Fraan had not looked particularly out of place behind his uncle's desk when I'd first seen him.

Yet, after the discovery of the body, he'd looked strangely immature for the task. Barely into his teens.

A young mind in an artificially matured body?

Plagiar had birth records. Had he ignored Fraan because he did not look the right age?

Fingerprints.

Fingerprints . . . and children.

Children. . . ! And institutions. . . ! And a man so obsessed with finding a particular child that he'd mounted an elaborate magic show so he could pursue his search from planet to planet, from institution to institution, under its suspicion-diverting cloak. Would such a man be capable of ignoring *any* boy, regardless of age, when all he needed to be sure was to check a fingerprint?

Or was it simply a case of checking the ready places first, and the nephew of a transhaus manager would have his turn, but in time.

Even if he hadn't known of Fraan until after Baas was dead, it was still simple enough to check the prints on anything the boy had touched . . . but the death of the uncle had brought the boy to the attention of the police and to spirit him out of sight was to act in the glare of an investigational spotlight . . . and big man or no, Plagiar was, after all, not a local . . . and he was sensitive. *That* he'd demonstrated to begin with by apparently feeling the need to use a magician's act as subterfuge.

Plagiar had his finger on the boy. All that he needed now was the patience to wait until the hue and cry died down.

And that brought the usefulness of the knowledge he thought I had to an end . . . and he no longer had a reason to keep me alive.

If Fraan was the boy they all sought, *nobody* had a reason to keep me alive . . . and any number of reasons to want me dead.

I had to know if the boy and Fraan were the same, to know if my ace-in-the-hole, blank though the card might be, had any value toward keeping me alive. It is one thing to bluff with a dud card in the hole ... it is another to try it when you do not even have a hand.

Fingerprints. It should be easy enough for me to get Fraan's if I did not already have them on the receipted transhaus bills in my pocket, but what to check them against?

Brigit might get to Plagiar's originals.

Brigit ... or the bully boy.

The bully boy whom I had clipped with his own gun, yet who had slipped me Brigit's note, he might....

Betrayal

No matter what you do, it leads to a betrayal. A betrayal of your own ignorance to Plagiar if he has already found a way to check the clerk and does not want him.

A betrayal of the lad's whereabouts and an end to the supposed secret you know is keeping you alive, if the prints match.

But you have to know.

You have to know.

Chapter Eighteen

The explosion was more a tremble in the ground than a sound in the air. I felt it, faint though it was, as I was coming into sight of the spaceport perimeter strip.

After the blast came a long, long stillness and then I saw the column of black, greasy-looking smoke begin to rise.

Slowly, lazily almost, straight up into Poldrogi's hot, motionless air from somewhere well beyond the low mud-brick buildings that hid the spaceport itself from my view.

With the smoke came a rush of people on either side of me and, as I swung onto the perimeter strip itself, from the distance and from nearby on the spaceport tarmac, the red and yellow emergency vehicles, all beeping their ear-shattering double-note, high-low, high-low, all streaking toward the rising column of smoke, now beginning to flatten out at the top as that part of it reached and mingled with the high-level thermal layer that turned Poldrogi's heat back down onto itself like the lid on a sizzling fryer.

I knew before I reached it what it was I'd find burning.

The transhaus.

Poldrogi has no department for fighting fires nor, for that matter, had any of the transit worlds I'd been on. That dirty job is by choice and agreement taken care of by the spaceport itself. The police, however, are a local force.

I spoke to a sweaty private in the brown-uniformed human line holding back a wavelike swarm of the curious.

"Hurt," I shouted to him over the din of the fire vehicles, the arrival of more police, the hoarse bellow of commands "Hurt, is there anyone hurt?"

He did not look at me, he rolled his dark eyes skyward. "Hurt," he said. "A transhaus blows up and he wants to know is there anyone hurt."

"The clerk," I shouted, and then I recognized the squat, red-faced figure of the police corporal in the midst of a small knot of standby police.

"Corporal," I shouted until I caught his attention; after staring at me a long moment with those cold eyes, he moved close enough for me to drop my voice.

"Corporal," I asked him. "The young clerk, Fraan, is he all right?"

He shrugged. "For the moment it would appear that the explosion originated in the manager's office. Whether the boy was in it or not at the time we have as yet no way of knowing."

He flicked his eyes to my wrist. "You are not wearing your timepiece," he said. "It is inside your compartment still?"

I nodded. It was. I hadn't the time or the chance to retrieve it.

"Then I can understand your concern," he said,

and he turned his back on me and left me to stare at the back of his red neck under the uniform cap.

The police brass were gathering. I saw captain's bars, lieutenant's, and now even the star of a police general. Did this cool the corporal's ardor for speech ... or was his dealing with me in this manner an idea all his own for solving the two murders he was saddled with?

Or, the thought suddenly struck me, did the corporal have his own designs on the wealth, the power, the "everything" Brigit had thought to tempt me with on the dark road behind the Wayfarer's Home?

Brigit.

A motion glimpsed out of the corner of my eye and when I looked, there she was, waving frantically to me, almost as she had from the Home parapet before the sniper's shot had whirred past me; waving from close behind the police line.

The corporal's back was still to me; I pushed my way toward Brigit and when she saw me coming, she at once began to edge out toward the rim of the crowd.

She was standing by the side of her twin-seated green and black skimmer by the time I caught up with her, her face looking genuinely frightened.

"Anton," she said, and her voice was almost a pant, "Anton will want to see you. Will you come?"

The note in her voice was new, and it struck me. This was not an order, it was not a wheedling, this was a request. One she obviously felt I might not be willing to agree to.

And what had brought that look of fright to her face?

I indicated the column of now richly billowing smoke with my head. "Does he know about this?"

"I don't think so ... I'm sure he doesn't ... it puts a whole new face on things. I *know* he will want to see you ... he *must* see you. Will you come?"

A new face on things. A transhaus blows up and suddenly my importance is so great that for Plagiar to see me, to talk to me is just as suddenly for him a must.

Go with her?

Go with her with so many loose ends, so many suspicions, so many scraps, but no more real knowledge than I'd had when I faced Anton Plagiar before...?

I searched my instincts, sought the counsel of the scar on my head, but that had been itching me for so long that, as a guide at this point, it was useless.

Abruptly, I got into Brigit's skimmer. I didn't know if I was obeying a deep-seated impulse ... or had seen and taken into account the black and white skimmer I saw coming to a stop nearby.

Near at hand, but still not close upon us because of the police blocking off traffic.

But by this time I was getting so that I could recognize Plagiar's blue and yellow bully boys at almost any distance.

Chapter Nineteen

We were headed for Plagiar's hostel, that much I could tell from the direction Brigit was taking. It was not far; I felt I had no time to waste. I plunged, hoping to perhaps make the fear I thought I saw in her face of some advantage to me. I needed all the edge I could get.

"This has happened before," I said, and the glance Brigit cast back at the pillar of smoke told me that I'd guessed right.

"Once," she said. "Once before, we thought we were close, and we barely escaped with our lives."

"We?" I said.

"Anton and myself," she said.

"Anton was here just now?" I said, knowing that only moments ago she'd talked as though he hadn't been, that he had to be told of the explosion.

Annoyance diluted the anxiety in her face. "Of course not. You make a great pretense of not knowing things that I am sure you do."

"I'm not pretending that I don't know what this is all about," I said.

"It is enough that you know where the boy is. To know anything more could be dangerous."

115

"I worry about it," I said. "I worry about things like more money than I can dream of ... and power ... and a man lying dead only yards from where I am being told of these things."

"Sklar was a fool," Brigit said. "A man well educated and fantastically knowledgeable in the history of thought ... of ideas. But he was a fool all the same."

"He is also dead," I reminded her. "It would be stupid of me to say anything with a second man murdered."

She chewed on that one a little bit. "I can tell you nothing," she finally said.

I reached out and cut the ignition tab; the skimmer dropped to the pavement and chattered to a rough stop.

"Good-bye," I said. "I don't plan on talking to Plagiar ... or to you ... or to anybody else until they let me in out of the cold."

She sat a moment in silence, then reached out a hand toward the tab. I caught it and held it in mine while the silence grew.

I broke it. "I have seen the boy," I said. For all I knew, I might have.

Her head snapped around, her eyes intent on my face.

"I have seen the boy," I repeated. "I want to know his real identity ... the reason Anton would offer fifty thousand Earthside dollars."

The steadiness of her eyes flickered and I felt her hand in mine go lax with resignation. I let go of it and reached for the ignition tab. Stopping was giving the bully boys a chance to catch up with us.

I flicked it on. The skimmer rose and now Brigit drove almost dejectedly.

"Don't take it so hard," I said. "What difference does it make if one more person knows?"

"Anton will kill me," she said, but she wasn't talking to me, she was talking to herself.

"You and Anton know. Who else?"

"Sklar, of course, but he is dead."

"Yes," I said. "And so is Mahar Baas."

"You knew. You knew who he really was." It was not a question.

I knew no more than what the police corporal had told me, but Brigit was giving me credit for knowing the much more that I hoped she would.

"Anton knows, and I know. Anton has been very careful to keep it from anyone else. He trusts his men to do what he tells them to. He does not trust human nature enough to tell them why."

I nodded but said nothing. When Brigit spoke, it was more to herself than to me. In her voice sounded the curious blend of relief and secretiveness of someone who has kept locked up inside herself a story she was burning to be rid of. Yet one she dared not broach even to the one other person who might also know it.

Brigit was plainly a woman with a bang-up story she'd kept penned up inside herself for too long a time.

I glanced back through the rear window of the tiny skimmer. They were there. At least I saw their black and white skimmer close behind us in the light traffic.

They were making no pretense that they were not following us. Plagiar's bully boys.

I studied the low buildings around us. I did not know the area all that well, but I had the feeling that we should be coming up on Plagiar's hostel at any moment.

I hoped that Brigit's story would not take longer in the telling than the time it looked like I had left in which to hear it.

Chapter Twenty

I turned in my skimmer seat to look at Brigit. "You," I said, "have got to be kidding."

She did not take her eyes from the street, the traffic in front of and around us. "It is true," she said. "He was looking to put together a biologically activated locking device, but what August Rook actually worked out was a way to transmit matter."

August Rook. The name was strange to me, but the idea of a matter transmitter wasn't. It was on a par with buckets of steam and left-handed monkey wrenches; with the philosopher's stone that was supposed to transmute base metals into gold; with the universal solvent that would dissolve everything ... except what would you keep *that* in once you'd found it.

No, the idea of transmitting matter was no stranger to me, or to anyone, and I couldn't see Anton Plagiar sucked into anything involving that goldbrick.

Yet Brigit was deadly serious, there could be no mistaking that. But a matter transmitter?

The theory of how one should work was simple enough. With sound, you took a voice, translated it into electrical impulses, and broadcast them. At the desired receiving point you picked up and retranslated the impulses into a fluctuating sound wave which, striking the ear of the listener, gave you the voice effect again.

With a visual image you did pretty much the same thing except that you dealt now with a pattern of light and shade for the eye rather than a fluctuating sound wave for the ear. You scanned your image pattern with what amounted to an electronic pencil at the pickup end ... and used another playing across the face of a cathode-ray tube to retranslate the values it had picked up into an image for the eye to see at the receiving end.

In short, select a point, gauge its value. Transmit your electronic evaluation to a receiver that will reproduce its intensity, its value in exact accordance with your electronic instructions ... and your viewer has his point of light to see. Repeat and repeat and repeat this gauging at incredible speed and the pattern of light intensities this makes on your screen will overlap and blend in the eye of your viewer until the image in his brain is one he perceives as being that of the thing, the person you are telecasting.

The mental gambit from transmitting an image to transmitting the thing itself is easy ... and all but inevitable.

For your scanning pencil, select a ray that will not only take note of the surface look of your thing, but be capable of going beneath that surface, of penetrating into your object itself.

Such "X" rays exist; it is only a question of devising one that can be focused to a fine degree, fine enough to scan your object atom by atom.

Atom by atom so that you can analyze and identify each and every atom contained in your object. Analyze and take note not only of its kind and composition, but also of its position within the specific form of your object.

This information you, of course, make available to your transmitter in the usual form of electronic impulses to be broadcast.

In your receiver you reverse the process, restoring every atom in its noted position, each atom of its noted kind. Restoring the look, the shape, the composition of your original object.

Simple.

Except that it is a far cry between the simple reading of a light value as reflected from a surface and the complete and thorough analysis of the atoms that make up that surface.

It is an even farther cry to repeating the same analysis for the billions and billions of atoms that lie, not only on that surface, but in the infinite layers beneath it until you have scanned, with your penetrating pencil, every single atom that makes up your object.

Yet Brigit was serious. I could not doubt that.

A confidence game? A deadly serious one if that was what it was. Two men had already died that I knew of. Were there others?

But assume the incredible. Assume that someone named August Rook had indeed found a way to not only analyze an object atom by atom but, what was even more incredible, more impossible of belief, that he had found a way to transmit this data and *restore* it to a tangible, a touchable, existence. That he could transmit an object. That he could translate a thing into an electronic pattern ... and then reassemble from a stock of necessarily unspecific atoms, perhaps even synthesizing the ones not readily at hand, its exact duplicate at any desired point.

That made my mind boggle. That, and what it implied.

The fact that a transmitter was not necessarily a transmitter alone. It could also be a duplicator ... and the number of duplicates depended not upon how many objects you were sending, but upon how many receivers you had picking up the signals.

That if you could broadcast a signal, you could also record it. And play back that record again and again and again ... and make duplicates of the record and thus increase your original object not simply one-to-one, but as close to a geometric progression as you wished to come.

August Rook, looking for a pilferproof lock, had destroyed the need for factories, for whole manufacturing industries, for warehousing facilities ... even for the fleets of cargo ships that gave the reason for existence to whole worlds, to whole strings of worlds.

Why ship anything if you could reduce its pattern to simple sheets as I did my camera's holograms, and then mail that pattern to its destination ... at rates that were already notoriously low?

Why make anything more than the one time you needed to make it for a recordable pattern?

Why ship it? Why even buy it when all you needed to possess it was access to its pattern on a bit of tissue-thin plastic.

My mind boggled. Boggled at the thought of a workable matter transmitter, boggled even more at the fantastic, the almost unintelligible, the frightening upheaval that would sweep over the galaxy when the import of its existence was realized.

Control! The thought of control swept into my mind ... and of the man who would control the secret of Rook's device.

That man would have in his hands a power the magnitude of which had never before been seen, been dreamed of, in all the histories of all the worlds of the galaxy.

That man, it was plain to me now, Anton Plagiar meant to be ... and the sweat on my face and running down my sides was suddenly cold as the immensity of the prize he meant to gain got through to me.

A prize to which he thought I had the key.

A prize Sklar and Baas had died for ... and a key I knew next to nothing about.

"The boy," I said, surprised to find myself a little breathless; surprised to find Brigit's sincerity catching at my belief, if only a little. "How is the boy involved?"

But we were already at Plagiar's hostel, Brigit slowing to look for her chance to cut across the traffic and into the yawning, black shadow that was the entrance to its parking area ramp.

Tell me. Before I face Plagiar again, I must know. Tell me about the boy. Tell me about the boy.

The bully boys were closing in on us now that we were at their home base. I had an instinct to run. I did not see myself meeting Plagiar in their company.

I thrust my feeling aside. Run? Our skimmer could not in any way outdistance their heavier powered one.

The street traffic. I saw an opening coming.

"Now," I said. "Now," and our skimmer shot through the small hole in the flow. A small hole, enough to let us dart through but not enough of a break to let the larger machine behind us do the same.

We swooped down the ramp into the relative darkness at its foot.

"Here," I said, bringing Brigit to a stop in a patch of shadow deeper, to my sun-accustomed eyes, than the general dimness of the underground expanse.

"Down," I said. "Get out and get down behind the cars here, and stay down. Hurry."

She was puzzled and she looked it, but she did drop down out of sight behind the row of parked vehicles I'd pointed to.

The hostel charged higher prices than the transhaus; it also gave its guests better service, providing two elevators for them at the far end of the parking area instead of a between-floors ramp.

I darted to the only one of the elevators ready and open. I stepped inside, pressed a button for the topmost floor, and darted out again as the doors started to close.

The empty elevator started its rise, the indicator above its doors slowly blinking off the first of its numbered floor indicators.

I ran back to Brigit and her concealing row of vehicles and dropped down beside her, signaling her to silence.

Time. I'd made it in time. The bully boys swept down the ramp in a flurry of rushing air, grated to a stop and ran for the second of the elevators even as their skimmer rocked with the roughness of its settling.

They reached its closed doors and the taller one

banged out his frustration against them with the flat of his left hand. His right, bandaged and stiff, identified him for me.

He shouted something to his companion that I didn't catch, but his meaning was clear enough. With his splinted right hand he was pointing toward the spiral fire-ramp at the end of the elevator wall.

They dashed for it together. At least they started to.

"Hold it."

The voice came from behind me and when, still squatting down, I turned my head, I saw the parking area attendant. A young man in blue coveralls stained indigo in spots by his sweat. And in his hand...

In his hand he held a small stun gun and he was pointing it not at the bully boys but at me.

At me crouched beside Brigit and against the row of skimmers he was responsible for.

"Stand up," he was saying. "Easy, very easy."

And as I rose up slowly, facing him, my arms held over my head so that he could see that my hands were empty, I heard the bully boys laughing.

Chapter Twenty-one

I looked at the bully boys who'd all but carried me up to his suite.

I looked at Brigit who seemed to be interested in a small red mark on the tip of one finger.

Last of all I looked at Anton Plagiar sitting behind a small, very ornate table of native wood that I hadn't seen the last time I was here. Before him was a thick sheaf of papers which he did not look up from when I was shoved into the room.

He spoke without raising his eyes, his fingers, holding a thin gold stylus, running the lines of the papers swiftly as he did so.

"The explosion. I've had news of it. Was it the boy?"

Brigit answered him.

"It was the same as the last time. No one had the chance to see anything."

Plagiar pondered that a moment and then he looked up at me, his fingers holding his place on the paper in front of him.

"You," he said.

A tiger. A tiger with the feel about him of impatience unleashing. His shock of white hair bristling. A white tiger.

"You, Pike, if you have anything to say, talk."

I took the plunge.

"Anton," I said, calling him by his first name. "I think we ought to be alone."

His eyes, steady on my face, did not move for a long moment. Then they shifted to look past me and the thin lips under the pencil mark of white mustache seemed suddenly to relax.

I caught the almost imperceptible nod of his head.

I caught the nod and felt at almost the same instant, on my right shoulder, between the tip and my neck, the chopping blow.

I felt the chopping blow and gasped with the unexpectedness of it and with the pain.

Pain, hot, intense, flooding my arm and my shoulder with the numb tingle of its paralyzing shock; making me blink with the fullness of its agony.

I was spun, sagging, half around, my hand gripping of itself my aching shoulder. Spun half facing the taller of the bully boys, my face to his patched one split in a grin from one side to the other.

His left hand. He must have chopped down on my shoulder with his left hand, his right still wore the splints and the bandages he'd earned when I broke his fingers with his own gun.

Weak. I felt weak as the pain in my shoulder began to ease ... or was I beginning to pass out from the intensity of it?

I tried to flex my fingers and I couldn't. I shook my head and felt the sweat that had burst from my forehead fly.

And I saw the bully boy's grin grow broader.

I saw it grow broader until there was nothing

before my eyes but those teeth and the muscular sweaty throat beneath them.

My hand.

My hand that was gripping my shoulder flattened and moved.

Flat it moved ... and edgewise. It moved the short distance from my pain-racked shoulder to his throat, to the front and a little below where it met the angle of his jaw.

He was lucky.

I was weak ... and it was my left hand. Had it been my right ... and moving with my full strength ... I might have crushed his voicebox.

He was lucky.

Had I known anything at all of what I was doing, my body would have had a practiced pattern in which to move of itself and he would have been a dead man, losing his fight to suck air through the wreck of his throat.

He was lucky. My blow only sagged him back against the closed door, his eyes popped and straining, his good hand clutching at his throat, his maimed one over it, the splinted fingers stiff, the three still free of bandages wrapped around their mates in a gesture almost pitiful in its futility.

He gagged. He gagged and he retched red and straining ... but he could breath.

He was lucky.

I was lucky.

I felt his partner's hand heavy on my shoulder, the fingers clawed and pulling.

I was lucky. Lucky that I was hurting too much to be thinking.

"Make it tough," I shouted at Plagiar. "Make it

real tough. Fifty thousand? Forget it. I want half. Half of everything . . . or forget it."

His hand with the gold stencil in it shot up. "Dvar," he said and the bully boy with his hand on my shoulder stopped in the middle of his yank at me.

"Dvar. Sit him down, over here." And the bully boy had his arms under mine and was letting me slip down into the broad chair to which Plagiar had pointed.

I did not try to hide my sagging. A near-miss from a masher beam and now this to help me get back my strength. I could not have concealed my sagging if I'd tried.

The taller bully boy was leaning against the wall on both his outstretched arms, head down, the retching sound growing less in his gasping. Neither Plagiar, nor Dvar . . . nor Brigit seemed to be paying him any mind.

Plagiar was handing me a glass. I could not have held it in my right hand, I did not reach for it with my left.

Brigit took it from him and held it up to my lips.

It was smooth, liquid smooth to the point of having almost no feel of its own . . . and it glowed. It glowed warmly all the way down.

Brigit set down the empty glass and now Plagiar waved to his bully boys. Waved them out of the room.

When they were gone, the one holding his throat, his breathing an audible wheeze, and leaning on the other, Plagiar sat looking at me a long, long moment, his fingers drumming on the tabletop.

"It would appear," he finally said, "that you do not take well to intimidation."

I was rubbing my shoulder; it ached, but not so much now that I felt I was going to pass out from it. And I wasn't about to tell him that my striking out at his bully boy had nothing to do with anything except the sight of that broad, broad grin in the middle of my hurting.

"It helps to bear the pain," I said, "if you know your man won't let himself go all the way."

Brigit cut in, talking to Plagiar. "He knows the boy."

I nodded. "That's right. I know the boy. I don't need his fingerprints or a photograph. I can spot him as soon as I see him."

Plagiar darted a glance at Brigit. "Then it *was* he at the transhaus."

I answered for her. "It was. And the place blew up as before."

I was telling him only what Brigit had told me, but in the telling, I was hoping that he would give me the natural credit for knowing more than I did.

I didn't feel the ground I was on would be any shakier for the attempt.

Plagiar's grin was suddenly wolfish. "You weaken your position, Pike. You have pointed the boy out to me. Why should I now let you live?"

"You weren't listening, Anton," I said, deliberately calling him by his first name again. "I told you I know the boy on sight. You don't. And the explosions make it clear, to me anyway, that you can't even get close to him without something blowing up. Me, I don't seem to have that problem. I've talked to him, remember."

For the first time I saw Plagiar show what I took to be a sign of uncertainty. He seemed to be chewing a corner of his mustache.

"If I could be sure," he finally said. "Sklar was a fool, but a wily one. I have only your word ... and my reports on him, that I have been following the right boy. Sklar could have deliberately meant to deceive me ... left a false trail ... the boy could be hidden elsewhere."

I had the answer to that one. At least I hoped I did. I used my left hand to take my wallet from my pocket, fish from it the latest of the transhaus receipts.

"If I haven't smeared them," I said, and I was hoping that by saying that I could copper my gamble if I'd reasoned wrong, "there should be a print or two on this that you might find interesting."

I tried to put a note of confidence into my voice ... but I wasn't sure I'd made it.

Plagiar took the receipt from me, laid it on the tabletop, pushing aside his papers to do so.

From an inside pocket of his tunic he took a flat round case about the size of a woman's compact. Opening it, he slid from it a gray, cookielike disk. There was a short handle clipped into the top of the carrying case, Plagiar did not bother with it.

From his wallet he took a shaded plastic rectangle and slid it under the flat clip that lifted up from the top of the gray cookie.

He touched a tiny lever on the edge of the disk and I heard a faint hum.

He moved the disk over the receipt like a man moving a miniature mine detector, and suddenly I saw him and his bully boys, and perhaps even Brigit, doing the same thing to fingerprint records in a Home office while a performance of magic was going on outside to divert the attention of the staff.

Maybe my camera-planted laser hadn't allowed

him the time to do the job on Poldrogi, but there must have been other places, other times, in which he'd thus searched for the trail of a boy he could know in no other way.

The hum changed to a tiny beep and back to a hum again.

Instantly, Plagiar came back to the edge of the receipt he'd just passed over and the beep returned to stay. It had located for him a latent print that matched the specimen he'd slipped under the clip on its top.

Plagiar put down his tiny detecting device. He started to get up, not bothering to mask the exultant gleam that had leaped into his eyes.

"It is the boy," he said. "Come, he must not get away again."

I stayed as I was. I didn't move.

"He isn't there," I said.

Plagiar stared blankly at me for a moment, then he dropped back into his seat. "Of course, the explosion. It masked his escape last time ... he'd have been gone before it was set off this time too."

He looked at me speculatively. "And you are gambling your life that I will not risk another such setback, but will make use of what is your one remaining asset ... that you alone know the boy on sight."

"It's not so great a gamble," I said, "when you consider the stakes. Half of ... of ..." Mindful of the value Brigit had set on it, I groped for a word to describe the magnitude of the prize the boy could lead him to and I couldn't find one. "... of the galaxy," I finished.

"You ask a high price for so simple a chore, Pike."

I shrugged. "I was hurting before when I said half. I'm not a pig. I'll take a third."

Plagiar chuckled. The same deep-down sound he'd made when the bully boy had leaned his shoulder into me and shoved the last time I'd left this room.

"A third. A third of all there is, all there ever will be, is not being a pig."

Then he was talking to me. "Pike, I think my promise to give you what you ask would not be believed by you. Why do you bargain?"

It was my turn to laugh. I hoped I made it sound real, If I didn't, I had a second hope that he'd figure my shoulder, which I was still hanging on to, hurt as much as ever.

"Anton," I said, "your promise is only part of what I want. I know the stakes, and I know the boy. But I don't know how to use the one to get the other. Tell me that and I'll take my chances that you will keep your word."

Plagiar did not need any time at all to figure that one. He held up three fingers, counting them off.

"One, the stakes. Two, the boy. Three, how to use him to get the stakes. I have one and three, you have one and two. I give you three, and you have all the parts to our little puzzle, while I am left with but my original two. And this, you think, will keep me honest."

"That's about it," I said.

I had no illusions about Plagiar's honesty, but I had a very large reason for wanting him to think that I was trying to protect myself on this point and that this was the way I'd figured to do it."

My real reason was much more basic. I wanted to keep breathing.

Somewhere I'd heard it said that he who would ride a tiger must be prepared never to dismount. And that's just where I felt I was. Astride a very large tiger.

Only I'd never chosen to ride it, still didn't know how I'd been euchred into it . . . and prize-of-the-galaxy or no, I wanted off.

Being big rich was one thing, being dead rich was another.

My nerves had been beam-shattered, my shoulder judo-chopped. But I was still breathing . . . and to keep that up I knew I had to keep this very dangerous man convinced that without me, he could not grasp his prize.

I heard him sigh. Deeply and loudly. Resignation?

Had Anton Plagiar decided to give in to what I hoped looked to him like the inevitable?

Or was he hoping to con me as I was desperately hoping to con him?

I could not know.

All I could know was that for him the stake was the wealth and the power of the galaxy.

For me, the stake was my life.

Chapter Twenty-two

Anton Plagiar had poured himself a drink of the warming liquid Brigit had held to my lips and was swirling it about in his hand. My shoulder was letting up its pain and numbness so that I could have held my drink in my right hand if I hadn't chosen to use my left. Brigit was settling herelf very decoratively in the smaller of the room's two sofas.

I knew that I had just about as much reason to relax as had that long-ago fellow with the sword hanging over his head. Damocles.

Maybe less. A hair doesn't have a brain, a sensitivity, a whim.

But I hoped my act was convincing. At any rate, there was nothing I could think of to do except to keep listening to Plagiar talk.

"I never met Rook," he said. "I have his story from Sklar. Sklar was his friend," and Plagiar laughed when he said that word. "His friend, the man he came to for advice, for help when he was troubled.

"Rook was like so many of our back-world people, given to much thinking, much brooding, much pondering upon the fact of his existence, much pondering upon the harshness, the poorness of a teacher's life."

A teacher! And I was sure I could have gambled and won that he'd taught on the same planet, at the same school, from which Baas and Sklar had come.

"Something simple," Plagiar said, "something universal, something everyone would need and buy. That is what it finally drifted into Rook's mind he would need to at least ease the harshness of life for himself, and for his wife and son.

"The proverbial better mousetrap was what Rook was after and for him it was a pilferproof lock. Small, installed without the bother of the usual wiring, operable only by its own key and never any other.

"Bioelectronics was his field of specialization, so it was only natural that he work within it in the thinking out of his lock.

"You know locks, Pike. They have to close when you want them to close and open when you want them to open, and not in between. Certainly not to someone else's key. That is what Rook thought he'd hit upon . . . a personal, private key . . . that could not be duplicated by anyone, that was possessed by no one else but the man who'd set the lock."

I could buy that. The man who thought to use a fingerprint believed his key was unique . . . but a photograph could open his lock . . . as could a lifted print.

A reading of the skin's potential had been added to insure that it was the living thumb that was presenting itself. But I knew of a way to overcome that, any photographer did . . . and anyone else who didn't mind a stained thumb could open the safe-box at the foot of my transhaus bunk.

It was troublesome, of course, but the answer to that was in how big a prize you expected to pilfer. The method was asininely simple. The thumb presented to the lockplate had to have a particular pattern of ridges and whorls. It also had to be living skin to satisfy that part of the key reading.

So, coat the photographic emulsion directly onto the skin of your thumb and print the wanted ridge pattern on it.

Now develop and fix your thumb as though it were an ordinary pre-laser, pre-electronic photo, and you have your pattern to be recognized, and living skin to demonstrate it is authentic. The lock is open to you.

Voices, retina patterns, many things had been tried as the operating key to a lock. But hoarseness could blow the one, and a retina-pattern-operated lock had been known to too often ignore an eyeball that was more bloodshot than the one that had closed it.

What had Rook thought of that could be so unique?

"Body cells," Plagiar was saying. "The somatic cells of the body."

Body cells! Bioelectronics, Plagiar had said, was Rook's field. The study of the electronic structure, of the electronic functions of living organisms.

"Soma cells!" I said.

"Yes, the somatic cells of the body. Rook figured, and rightly so, I suppose, that nothing could be more unique to a man than the chromosome pattern of his body cells, and he started with that as his key."

"Lord, to analyze a body cell down to the last speck of its substance." I shook my head at the magnitude of the task.

Plagiar shrugged. "Until we can get his trunk open, who knows how he did it. Maybe he wasn't analyzing the substance at all, maybe he was working on energy patterns, electrical charges. Every man approaches his problem from the perspective of his own knowledge."

The trunk, I said to myself, remembering the upended service trunk look of the card-producing taboret that Brigit and the bully boy had rolled into the room the last time I'd been here. If that was Rook's trunk that Plagiar had, why didn't he break it open if he wanted what was inside it?

Unless the taboret wasn't masking the trunk ... or there was a good reason, a compelling reason, why he couldn't.

But I wanted the whole of his story. I didn't interrupt him with a question that was so obvious it could be taken as stupid. Nor did I want to break the flow of his words.

I nodded my agreement with his sally about the starting point of a man's problem-solving approach and let him talk.

"Rook had a head start on the device he needed to gather the initial cell sample. It was already a part of his work to slice specimens into incredibly thin slices for analysis. He had only to adapt his existing equipment to a shape and a size he could use with his lock."

I restrained the nod I felt myself about to give. I remembered the rubbing sensation at the tip of my finger when I'd placed it on the coin-sized disk atop the taboret. It *had* to be Rook's trunk Plagiar was masking.

"Rook was working for simplicity of installation, with no wiring between the lockplate that picked up and analyzed his cell sample, and the lock that recognized it. So, of course, he used a transmitter on the one, and a receiver on the other.

"According to Sklar, he intended to miniaturize his components when he had his principle worked out; meanwhile he was using whatever came to hand, paying no attention to its size or weight, which made for a bulky apparatus. Then, too, he had to keep his things somewhere safe and separate from the equipment that belonged to the university...."

"So he kept them in a trunk that he could lock," I said, forgetting for the moment my intention not to interrupt.

Plagiar nodded. "Yes, he couldn't work on his lock all the time, he had a living to earn ... and he was getting questions and some poking around from people from whom he was cadging his parts; asking for information he needed that was outside the scope of his own special field."

"Baas and Sklar," I said.

"Bass, but not Sklar. Sklar was his friend. Rook came to him only after he realized what it was that he had."

Again Plagiar laughed when he said the word friend.

I had it! Unbidden, while I was listening to Plagiar, it came together in my head. The scraping feel of cells being collected from my thumb ... a tranmitter ... and a receiver. I had it and I had to say it before Plagiar could.

"He had a working transmitter of matter ... or

a duplicator, whichever way you wanted to look at it," I said.

I said it calmly, as though I'd known it all along.

Plagiar looked at me a long moment over the rim of his glass before he spoke.

"You were not bluffing when you wanted my men out of the room. You really do know what is at stake."

I shrugged, wincing as the motion reminded me of the soreness of my shoulder. "If you didn't think that from the very first, you wouldn't be telling me Rook's story now."

Plagiar went back to toying with his glass, nearly empty now. "That is true. And then perhaps it is not. I could be amusing myself by telling you all with the full intention of killing you before you can repeat it to anyone else."

It was a possibility, but I wasn't about to add to the pressure my scar and my brain were already under by giving it to them to consider.

I came as close to a snort as I ever do. "I figure that if it's kicks you want, you've got better ways of getting them," and I could only hope that I was right.

Plagiar's laugh sounded genuine enough to me, but all the same I was in no position to feel easy about it.

"I have said it before, Pike, you do not take well to intimidation."

It might look that way from where he sat, but he didn't have a scar on the top of his head to tell him different, a scar he was aching to scratch and didn't dare to.

Aloud I said, "Rook didn't know he had a matter transmitter until when?"

"Not until his basic unit was complete and operating. He discovered its full usefulness only when he got to testing it."

I remembered that Sklar was an associate in philosophy. A man might seek the help of a philosopher friend if in his mind he was wrestling with something big ... something overwhelming. And Plagiar said that Rook went to Sklar for help.

"And the thought of all that loot in his grasp flipped him?" I said.

"Not just then. You must remember that Rook went to work on his transmitter not for money itself, but for the new life he hoped money would bring him ... and his wife and son. A man with that kind of a mind may find huge sums of money pleasant to think about, but that contemplation doesn't—how did you put it?—doesn't flip him. Rook was excited, of course, greatly so, if Sklar was to be believed, but only excited."

"You said he found out what he had only when he came to test it."

"Yes. He told Sklar that he had the unit set up and working when it dawned on him that he'd thought himself right past any real, any practical, usefulness his device may have had.

"You see, he'd wanted a lock that would open to only the one key ... but he'd picked a key so exclusive that only one individual in the galaxy could open his lock once it was closed ... and that he had to do it in person."

I got Plagiar's point, and I could imagine the dismay that must have poured over Rook when the same thought struck him. A lock with one key ... and one that you had to open personally was fine. But it went too far. You wanted security, but you didn't want to have to drop whatever you were doing to go open a lock whenever someone who had to get past it wanted in.

You wanted a secure key, but one you could also hand to someone else, a key you could leave behind if you needed to be elsewhere, a key you could send in your stead ... and you couldn't have it with Rook's lock. It was a great idea, but it had its real and obvious limitations.

"When the thought struck Rook," Plagiar was saying, "he wondered if other things beside a body cell could operate his lock. He had a pencil in his hand ... a metal mechanical one ... he touched it to his pickup button ... and his unit shorted out.

"He tore it apart to find the trouble ... and that was when he found the bits of metal in his lock. Microscopic, but bits of metal.

"He was puzzled. They looked like ... and they checked out to be ... bits from his pencil tip ... but he hadn't had it anywhere near the inside mechanism of his lock.

"It was then he realized that his receiving unit wasn't just picking up and identifying the pattern of impulses the lockplate was sending to it ... it was reproducing them also. The body cells he'd been sending through it so far hadn't shorted it ... but the first bit of metal had."

I don't know if I'd have flipped if I'd had all that potential loot staring me in the face, but Plagiar'd said that Rook hadn't.

"If that didn't flip him," I said, "what did?"

"He was a biologist ... living organisms ... he had to know if he could move something that was alive as well as something that wasn't.

"Rook's equipment was by this time getting to

be fairly sophisticated and the questions it raised were getting hard to ignore, according to Sklar. But Rook was eager and he thought he'd found the weak part in his devising.

"His sample-collecting unit. He'd adapted it from a specimen slicer so that in essence what it did was no different from what a meat slicer might do in a packaging plant, and while he could hold a bit of metal or plastic in contact with his pickup until it had shaved off as much as he cared to send, he couldn't do the same thing with anything alive and expect to end up with anything more than a bloody pulp.

"Speed was the answer, Rook felt. A mechanical knife could be made to move only so fast, but a beam of light. . . .

"A beam of light could be made to play over an object so rapidly that the tiny point of its moving could look, to the eye, like a broad flood illuminating the whole of it.

"A cutting beam of light moving at what, for it, was a not impossible speed ... perhaps it could strip away and scan the whole of an organism in the fraction of its heartbeat."

"It worked," I said.

"It worked," Plagiar said. "With a virus. The first living thing that Rook sent that was able to survive the trip from his pickup to his receiver was a tobacco mosiac virus. It had no heartbeat, but it was a living entity ... and the potential of what he had done ... the moral consequences of his discovery ... preyed on Rook's mind ... sent him looking for an answer ... for help from his friend whose special field was the study of truth ... of underlying principles ... of philosophy."

"Sklar," I said.

Plagiar nodded. "Sklar. Rook was looking ahead. Far ahead. He felt that once he'd demonstrated the possibility of transmitting *any* life, it was only a question of application, of engineering, of time, before someone would work out a way to transmit a man. And *that* is the consequence that troubled him . . . the consequence over which he brooded."

It was enough to give any man pause . . . a sensitive man hung on the one horn that meant wealth and power for him and his family . . . a legacy such as no man had ever left before . . . and the second and moral horn that spelled out potential chaos . . . a legacy also such as no man had ever left before, but of anarchy.

It was not hard for me to imagine the turmoil that, hung on these horns, must have been seething in Rook.

Outright murder, wholesale and in unending number, was only part of Rook's dilemma. To analyze his specimen to transmit it, he had to slice it into its component atoms, destroy it.

With an object it made no moral difference. You destroyed a pencil? You plucked its identical copy from inside your receiver. Or its duplicate repeated end on end until you had all the pencils you could possibly use.

But a man.

Was the man who emerged from your receiver the same man you'd sliced to infinity?

He was?

Then who is this other who is stepping from your second receiving unit? And the third . . . and the fourth?

And remember, if you can transmit an impulse, you can record it.

This bit of plastic which carries your directed pattern. You feed it into your transmitter and somewhere a pencil emerges.

This second bit of plastic. You feed *it* into the unit of your devising ... and a man steps out.

Is the plastic bit a man? Were you to destroy it, would you have committed a murder? Or did you already do that when you made your initial recording?

When you recorded your man.

When you *recorded* your man.

Have you achieved the ultimate depersonalization of a human being?

You have said the words before, when you'd taken down a man's name, his service number, his activities, his ancestry even ... and written them on a card....

You've said that you had him down in your file ... that he was to you a number on a bit of paper.... "I have him on my card."

But, of course, everyone, yourself included, knew you were only using an expression ... speaking an analogy....

But this bit of plastic you now hold in your hand...?

But murder ... ultimate depersonalization ... they are only on the rim of the potential; of the chaos.

Two men with an equal and identically valid claim to a piece of property ... blood brothers have destroyed each other for what each coveted of the other's possessions.

Covet the other's possession?

Impossible here. How can I covet what is mine own? This other self ... must I share of my substance with him? And this third ... and fourth? Lord, there will be nothing left of mine for me.

"Ladies and Gentlemen ... The President of ... Mr. President? Mr. President. Which of you is the President...?"

"Yes, Ma'am. Three boys all exactly to your pattern. Delivery? Well, we're a little rushed...."

"Sir, we do not find your attitude at all reasonable. After all, is this or is this not *your* signature?"

"Dear Madam: We deeply regret to inform you of an unfortunate accident with reference to your order for three boys. Our equipment is of the finest and rarely does it jam. We realize the burden the fifty-four copies of your order places upon you and have contacted your Congressman...."

Yes, even a man of small imagination might flip ... and Rook's imagination was anything but small.

Aloud I said, "It's enough to make any man brood, let alone a man like Rook."

Plagiar shrugged. "There are men ... and then there are men."

I nodded. I couldn't agree more.

Plagiar went on. "At any rate, he went to Sklar for advice to help him make up his mind.

"Of course, Sklar didn't believe the fantastic story Rook was trying to tell him, and I suppose by now Rook wasn't any too coherent about it ... so Rook took Sklar back to his lab to prove to him that he wasn't hallucinating."

"Sklar believed him, then?"

"Sklar believed him ... and in his excitement he said things to Rook he told me later he never would have if he'd been able to keep his head. At any rate, he said Rook suddenly started shouting at him that he'd made his decision and tried to throw a vial of acid ... or a thermal cap ... Sklar wasn't clear what it was except that he knew Rook meant to destroy his transmitter.

"He panicked, he said. He had to stop Rook, and he did. But he said he didn't realize what he'd done until he saw Rook on the lab floor with his head smashed in and he, Sklar, standing there with a heavy glass pestle in his hand.

"There'd been noise ... and now he heard someone coming. He said his one thought was to hide Rook's body and he did ... in the only place ready and available to him in the few seconds time he had left."

"In the trunk," I said. "He shoved Rook into his own trunk and slammed it closed."

Plagiar nodded. "Into the trunk with his transmitter, closed the trunk, and slid it the few feet he needed to cover the blood from Rook's head on the floor."

"He made it, then."

"Yes and no. The person he'd heard coming was a lab assistant working late...."

"Baas," I said.

"Baas. Sklar said all he could think of then was to get out of the lab and away. And he did. After all, the trunk was not something strange to the lab ... and Sklar was an associate there and known to Baas as a friend of Rook."

"But he went back," I said.

"He went back. He couldn't put the thought of the prize Rook had shown him out of his mind. So he went back, cleaned the floor of blood, and got Baas to help him to his quarters with the trunk, telling him Rook had been called away and had asked him, Sklar, to hold his trunk for him."

I remembered what I'd seen of Sklar and his jumpiness, and I could see a good reason for it. He had his own dilemma goring him with its horns.

Ditch the trunk and you ditch with it all the wealth of the world . . . keep it close and you keep close the instrument of your own doom, should it be opened.

"Opened," I said. "Did Sklar get rid of Rook's body?"

Plagiar shook his head. "Rook normally kept his equipment, his notes, everything together in the trunk when he wasn't working on it. When he became upset, he took even greater precautions that his transmitter not be tampered with. Not get out and into other hands while he was making up his mind about it. He not only secured his trunk with his unique lock, but he'd told Sklar that he'd fitted it with a device that would destroy the trunk and its contents should an attempt be made to open it in a way other than by its own lock. He was not specific, but Sklar believed him. He did not try to open the trunk."

"Then . . . then . . ." I said, dumbfounded, and pointed with my good arm at the doorway I'd seen Brigit and the bully boy emerge from wheeling a magician's taboret that reminded me of a trunk set up on its end, ". . . then you have . . . you still have. . . ?"

Plagiar looked at me a long moment and then he sighed. "I sincerely would like to know how much you know yourself and how much you arrive at by observation and guesswork."

He nodded. "Yes, I have Rook's trunk and his body is still inside it."

And now I understood Plagiar's impatience, too. It didn't make my shoulder feel any the better, but at least I could assign a reason to his testiness.

"But if the trunk is booby-trapped, and Rook's body is inside it ... and the lock is keyed to respond only to his body cells, how. . . ?"

My voice trailed off as I contemplated the complete bind into which Sklar's moment of panic had put him ... and Plagiar and, indirectly I suppose, me.

"The trunk isn't keyed to Rook's cells," Plagiar said. "He couldn't use his own cells to activate his equipment. He was working with it all the time, touching it, scraping his skin against it, dry cells sloughing off. No, if he used his own cells he could never tell if the activating cell came from his touch on the analyzer's button or from a random one that had fallen into the works.

"He had to key his lock to the cells of someone who was not normally in the lab, yet someone available to him now and for the future ... someone close."

I didn't need him to spell it out for me any further. "His son," I said. "Rook keyed the lock to his son's touch."

And now I had the answer to my why ... why they wanted a boy so badly that fifty thousand was only an amount flung out impatiently; and why Sklar could lie in a road with his head bashed in ... and Baas be sprawled and laser-lanced in a transhaus storeroom.

Suddenly, my close scrape with a masher beam was more than the memory of something past ... it was a chilling promise of the future.

Chapter Twenty-three

The transhaus, I meant to go back to it.

Back to it and the one way I could think of to get in touch with the boy.

But I meant to go alone. Not with Brigit, and certainly not with either of the bully boys in the skimmer following ours, the one bully boy easy to pick out by the white flash of his bandaged hand.

"It is of some consequence to me that you not be harmed," Plagiar had said to me. "To provide you with a small escort is the least I can do to ease both our minds."

Ease my mind ... I didn't know who'd killed Baas or Sklar ... and I didn't know and couldn't guess who'd had a try at me with a masher beam ... so that the prospect of a bodyguard should have been comforting.

But I couldn't help but wonder about the protectiveness of the bully boy who had a broken hand, a patched-up face ... and now a granddaddy of an aching throat to bring out his warm regard for me.

And I didn't kid myself that Plagiar's "guards" were anything other than a pair of not-too-happy-with-me jailers.

As usual, Brigit was driving, and I indicated the skimmer behind ours with a motion of my hand. "Your friend who gave me your note," I said, "is he with Plagiar ... or does he have ideas of his own?"

"I do not understand," Brigit said, but her voice did not carry any note that would convince me.

"I break a finger for him, yet he slips me your note to meet you out near the Wayfarer's Home. And he risks doing it right under Anton's nose. Why?"

She shrugged. "He is a good friend."

"That may be," I said, "but you don't take the chance of crossing a man like Anton out of friendship alone."

She did not change her line. "He is a good friend."

From the sound of her voice, I was rubbing the wrong way, but it told me what I needed to know. Any idea I might have had brewing about enlisting Brigit's help in getting clear of the bully boys behind us I could forget. And to break and run when next she slowed the skimmer down to where I could leap from it without smashing myself up was to make it clear to Plagiar what I had in my mind to do.

And unsuspecting was what I had to keep Anton Plagiar until I'd had my chance to make contact with the boy ... and to make a clean break ... or at least one that had a more promising start.

"Sklar had a fortune in his hands, and also a body he couldn't dump," I said. "I can see him asking around for a way to exploit the one, but I don't see him blabbing about the other. How did Anton get his hands on the trunk? From Baas?"

"No," and she sounded relieved. I made a mental note to dig a little deeper, if I got the chance, at the connection between her and Broken-fingers behind me.

"No, Sklar came to Anton himself."

"That I find hard to believe," I said. "He knew his murder of Rook would be out the moment Anton opened the trunk."

"You do not believe me? Then I can tell you that you have not observed Anton very closely."

She paused for a long moment, then added, "Were you aware that at one time Anton was a grunt-monkey in an opal mine?"

A grunt-monkey in an opal mine.

That was work as backbreaking and as dirty as the name implied. The opal is a strange stone, steeped in omen and superstition. No outfit of size or good sense would take the men or the machines to either synthesize or hunt out the few stones there was a market for.

But although the opal market was small and uncertain, it did exist, and a man could eke out an existence of sorts digging out the stones.

But heavy mining equipment, both the shipping and the carrying of it was out of the question. The opal hunters dug for them with their hands. It was grunt work in every sense of the word.

Grunt work that killed as many in collapsing mines as died for lack of food, or water, or air in the harsh regions in which they sought the gems.

And Dr. Rolf Sklar, associate in philosophy, had tried to tangle wits with a man who'd survived the opal digs and, if surface appearance had any meaning, had prospered.

But I did not believe that it was Plagiar who'd

killed him. The time for Anton to have done that was when he'd first latched onto the trunk.

"I believe that Rook's body in the trunk wouldn't keep Anton from making capital of whatever else might be in there with it. And I don't believe Sklar would look up somebody else to share with him in the opening."

"Tell me, of what use was Rook's device to Sklar as it was? All he had was a laboratory model and a handful of notes. Where were the money, the resources, the technical skills to take the notes and the model and to develop their potential?"

Brigit shook her head. "Poor Rolf. He was like a man carrying a soap bubble in a hot wind ... and going out of his mind with the fear of being discovered while seeking the right person to do for him what he could not do for himself. And then there was Baas."

Baas. Baas who had helped Sklar carry the trunk to his quarters the night he'd killed Rook.

"Baas knew?" I asked.

"Sklar told Anton that Baas had come to him the next day ... after Rook had not showed up for his classes ... and asked many questions."

"Blackmail," I said.

"Not then, Sklar said. He said Baas just asked many questions about Rook, when Sklar had last seen him, when he'd been told to take care of the trunk, things like that. Questions Sklar knew would be the ones the police would ask him, and he took it to mean that Baas was being very careful, but that he was letting him know that his presence must be considered.

"At least that was Sklar's impression then. Baas made it plainer the next time he came to him. Then he left no room for doubt. He wanted in, but by that time poor Rolf no longer had the trunk."

"Anton had . . . acquired it?"

"It was a misunderstanding all around," Brigit said. She looked over her shoulder, almost as though she was fearful of the bully boys in the skimmer behind us overhearing what she was about to say.

"Anton meant merely to take advantage of Sklar's presence in his office to make sure that no harm came to the trunk while they were . . . negotiating terms."

"You mean that while Anton kept Sklar busy, his bully boys burgled Sklar's place for the trunk."

I laughed. "Did Anton know at the time that he . . . he took the trunk into protective custody, did he know that it couldn't be opened?"

"Not exactly. I'm afraid Sklar was not entirely open with Anton. He'd told him what was in the trunk, but not that he needed Rook's boy to open it, or that Rook had booby-trapped it."

"It must have been a taut moment when Anton found out," I said.

"It was not a good moment for him," Brigit said. "He'd thought to confound Sklar and had the trunk brought in the moment Dvar and Hort arrived with it. He'd expected Sklar to panic and Rolf did . . . but only with fear that Anton would attempt to open the trunk."

"The boy," I said. "Anton did not try at once for the boy?"

"There was no point to it. It would appear that Sklar had taken the precaution of having Baas spirit the boy off-planet before he approached Anton."

"Sklar trusted Baas with the boy?"

"It was a small risk that he ran. Baas was an accessory now, and as deeply responsible in the guilt of Rook's slaying as was Sklar himself. Then, too, Sklar had the trunk. The boy was of little use without it."

That was true enough, and I could see Sklar, a quiet and philosophical man until his sudden confrontation with the vision of endless wealth and power brought him to impulsive murder and gutted his life's teachings of any meaning.

"But the boy's mother," I said. "Baas and Sklar surely didn't dare risk the outcry of an outright kidnapping at just that time."

"Remember that to August Rook's wife, Sklar was a close friend of her husband's. And Rook had been tense and worried. That he was a moody man was a secret to no one. Sklar had little difficulty persuading her that it would be best for the lad's sake for him to be sent elsewhere until the worst of what had happened to his missing father was known. Then, too, Baas was no stranger to the boy, but someone he knew through Baas' association with his father."

I remembered how Plagiar had started to his feet to go after the boy at once when his fingerprint detecting device had found and identified the print on the transhaus receipt I'd given him. I did not see him wasting time in taking off after Baas and the boy. I said as much to Brigit.

"It is a large galaxy in which to track down someone who is resourceful and determined you will not find him," Brigit said. "But Anton is not without his resources. Baas and the boy were not difficult for him to trace, but we did keep running into one setback after another.

"Sklar may have been lying to Anton, been fearful of having him catch up with the boy, but he claimed that Baas was not following his instructions as he had given them to him. I think Sklar was as surprised as anyone when a bomb blew out the doors and windows of the room Anton and his men were closing in on, and both Baas and the boy were able to break clear of us."

"But you found the trail again," I said.

"Yes, and this time we were more careful. For some reason, Baas seemed to be growing desperate. Had his bomb been better arranged it would have killed anyone who stepped into the room. As it was, no one was hurt."

Now a second bomb had been set off. But Baas was dead when this one blew. Had the boy found a new friend . . . or was he now acting on his own?"

With Baas, he had not been able to lose Anton. Without Baas, the boy's chances of escape seemed surely to have evaporated.

Doubly so, in Anton's mind, now that he had me to spot the boy on sight . . . and the spaceport's routine search-robot stowaway patrol to keep him on-planet.

I had to get away from Brigit and the bully boys for a quarter of an hour, at least . . . and I had to do it in a way that looked natural, that would stir no questions in Plagiar's mind.

Brigit would not be difficult. I had only to find a rest room with a back door I could slip out of and back in through to be free of her, but the bully boys. . . .

Fifteen minutes free of the one I'd heard Plagiar call Dvar, and his broken-fingered buddy, Hort.

Fifteen minutes free of their seeing me and, more importantly, of their hearing me ... and free in a way that would not bring down Plagiar's ire.

Fifteen minutes to set myself up with a boy who'd just demonstrated an unsettling association with explosives.

Chapter Twenty-four

The transhaus. We'd reached it, Brigit bringing our skimmer to the grating stop I'd come to expect of her, and I still had not thought of a way, had come upon no opportunity to escape the surveillance of Plagiar's bully boys.

The billowing of smoke was gone, but the bite of it was still strong in the air. Two of the spaceport's brightly yellow fire vehicles were still on guard, their chemical hoses snaking across the walk, up the single broad step, and into the transhaus itself, the revolving door jammed partly open on them.

The police lines were still in place, the big brass gone, the crowd thinned but milling.

The sight of the fire hoses piled one atop the other so that all could be crowded through the narrow aperture of the transhaus door ... and the light pressure of my record camera in its pocket on the left sleeve of my jumpsuit.... Had I found my way to be free of the bully boys?

"You stay here," I said to Brigit. "I want to get a picture of the crowd to study."

I ducked under the arm of a police private before Brigit could ask what I was about, and darted for the pile of hoses in the doorway.

A picture of the crowd to study. It was standard procedure to photograph the onlooking crowd at fires simply for the record. Thus later, should evidence of arson be found, the shot could be matched against others taken at similar fires in the hope of finding a face common to all. The one face that had a demonstrably good chance of being that of the arsonist held in thrall at the scene of his crime.

I did not think that the boy, Fraan, was under any such compulsion, but I had the start of my covering excuse for breaking away ready for Plagiar should I need it.

Onto the piled-up hoses I clambered, being as awkward about it as I dared be. A shout. Behind me I heard a shout and hoped it to be from the police private under whose restraining arm I'd darted.

I gave it no heed, but turned at the top of the pressed-in pile of hoses and fumbled for my camera.

I had it up to my eye and filming before I felt hands upon me. I shook myself free, hoping to steam the private.

I made it. His grip on me was firm and there was no getting away from him when I let him pull me down.

"It's nothing," I shouted to Brigit. "They can't hold me. I've got a right to do what I'm doing." I looked at Plagiar's bully boys, but their faces were too distant for me to make out how they were responding to the police taking me into custody.

"Inside," I said to the private, keeping my voice low. "Take me inside, and find your corporal for me. Hurry."

He eyed me with suspicion plain in his manner.

I repeated it. "Inside, and get your corporal. Hurry, please."

I think the unexpectedness of the "please" did it. He shoved me up over the pile of hoses and inside the transhaus. I hoped I looked unwilling to whoever was watching me.

The corporal was in the ruins of the manager's office and I saw his head come poking out even as I blinked at the choking, eye-smarting stench. The damage seemed confined mostly to that small room.

"Corporal," I said, "could we hurry? I haven't much time."

"This man," the private beside me had started to say, but the corporal waved him to silence.

"I will take care of it," he said, and the private let go of my arm and turned toward the doorway.

"Wait," I said to the corporal. "Could he stay inside for the moment? I don't want someone outside to see him and start to wonder what became of me."

The corporal nodded to the private and the man stayed. The corporal's eyes were on me. "You said you had little time," he said. "Little time for what?"

I motioned him to come with me as I headed for the down ramp leading to my sleep cubicle. I came right to the point.

"Rolf Sklar and Mahar Baas. I think I can give you their killer."

I didn't know if I could. I didn't know if it was one killer or two who had committed the crimes. But I said the one thing I hoped would hook the corporal.

"You were here when Baas was killed ... and you found Sklar on the road ... or so you say. Am

I to understand that you now wish to confess to both of these murders?"

I broke my stride, but only barely. "Good Lord, no." And the dismay in my voice was so plain that it struck clearly even in my own ears.

The corporal showd me his carved teeth. "So, my sitting duck has had some hunters let fly at him, then . . . and he has recognized a face?"

"No," I said. "But I do know things now that I didn't know before, but I need a little clear time."

We were at my sleep cubicle now. I thumbed the lockplate, waited for the ding of recognition and when it came, took out not my big camera but my wrist-chrono.

I started to put it into my inside pocket. It hadn't been on my wrist before; I didn't want Plagiar to wonder when or how I'd been able to escape surveillance to come by it.

I started to put it into my pocket, but then I shrugged. I could hide what I meant to do from the corporal, but now that he could listen in on me any time he wished to, might even monitor me around the clock, I could not hide my doing of it.

I held my timepiece up to my face. "Fraan," I said into it, "this is Eli Pike. You are within range of my voice, that much I am sure of. You are in great danger, that much I think you know. I know why. Repeat, I know why. We must both escape. Repeat. We must both escape."

I was keeping my voice as matter-of-fact as I could, gambling the double gamble that it *had* been Mahar Baas who had lightly drugged me and planted the transmitter in my wrist-chrono, and that Fraan, having adopted Baas' technique of blasting when closed in on, would also have taken the older man's receiver with him when he ran.

A rendezvous with the boy was what I was hoping to arrange.

It did not escape me for a moment, although I was doing pretty good at keeping it out of the front of my mind, that if it had been the boy who'd blasted the transhaus office, he might very well take me up on a meeting and set up the same kind of surprise for me when I showed up to keep it.

"Fraan," I said. "we must meet and escape together. Repeat. We must meet and escape together. I will be here," I said naming as the place, my sleep cubicle for the double reason that it was the only place I was sure both of us knew and that it might have some element of psychological persuasiveness for the boy. He'd escaped from the transhaus once, he might feel he could do it again if I planned a trap.

And also, would Plagiar look first for him right where he'd just run from?

"Do not signal me," I said, fearful that if he tried to acknowledge my call, he might be seen and taken.

"Do not signal me. Twelve hours," I said, making the calculation in my head for a time when we might have the cover of Poldrogi's black night. "Twelve hours. I will be here in twelve hours. Until then, do not let yourself be seen. Repeat. Do not let yourself be seen."

"The boy," the corporal said, "he is wanted for interrogation about the fire. I must warn you that my men will be here to pick him up."

I grabbed the sides of my balding head. My timepiece was still in my hand. If he was listening,

Fraan would have heard the corporal and there went any chance I might have had of his getting in touch with me.

The corporal treated me to the sight of his teeth again. He brought his hand out of his tunic pocket and I saw in it the small gray box of his signal damper, its amber light aglow. "After all," he said, "I did not know what you were about to say or to whom. I could not just let you talk."

I nodded, but he'd cost me precious minutes. "Repeat it," I said. "I must repeat it. And you cannot station your men here or anywhere nearby. The boy will see any change of routine and stay away."

I did not mention the possibility of his men being blown away by a bomb blast if that was the way Fraan meant to play it.

I wasn't being noble. What I didn't want was a bomb safety squad swarming over the building and its subterranean passages, searching for an explosive device that might or might not be there, to keep the boy at a distance.

"I cannot permit that he go unquestioned," the corporal said. I glanced at my timepiece. How much longer would Brigit and the bully boys stay topside without taking action to find out what had become of me?

"Time," I said to the corporal. "I do not have time. Keep your men away and I will bring the boy to you."

I said it, and I half believed myself when I did.

The corporal had not turned off his scrambler, its amber eye mocking me. Time, I had all but run out of time.

"Think of this," I said. "If your men are here, he surely will not come. If you stay away completely, you at least have the chance that I can bring him to you. It is a small chance against no chance at all."

The corporal chewed on that a moment and I became very conscious of the smarting of my eyes, the smoke bite in my throat ... of the sweat streaming down my sides and dripping from my face.

"Done," he said. "But I must warn you of the risk you take. I will not be easy with you if you are trying to deceive me."

He would not be easy with me ... *he* would not be easy with me if I had deception in mind.

What would the boy and his explosives do if he had the same idea about me?

What would Plagiar do?

The amber eye of the corporal's signal damper winked out: he'd turned the unit off.

I brought my timepiece back up to my lips. "Fraan," I said. "This is Eli Pike. I know that you are within range of my voice...."

The *corporal* was going to make trouble for me. If I'd been less pressed for time, I would have laughed.

Chapter Twenty-five

I thumbed the magnification of my viewer to its highest level to be sure I was seeing what I was seeing. I hoped that, held up to my eye, the unit had masked enough of my face to hide my start of surprise from Anton Plagiar, from Brigit, from the bully boys.

There were more of Plagiar's blue and yellow clad stocky young men now in the suite than just the two, Dvar and Hort. A kind of palace guard, I surmised. Not as many as had been swarming the Wayfarer's Home, but three pairs of them.

Three pairs who did not even pretend to be doing anything but taking turns at keeping me under constant watch.

Twelve hours, I'd told Fraan. Meet me in twelve hours.

With the transmitter in my inside pocket, its sensitivity unknown to me, added to the strain of waiting for darkness, I now had the further worry of keeping outside its pickup area the voices, the sounds, that might nullify the appeal I'd sent out to Fraan.

If I was lucky, that is; lead him to think me an enemy best dealt with by a third bomb, if I wasn't.

I didn't know how sensitive the transmitter in my watch was; could only guess at the limits of its pickup area.

But I did know what my camera shot, taken from atop the pile of hoses in the transhaus doorway, had just shown me.

I'd made the shot as a subterfuge, a device to get me out of the bully boys'—and Brigit's—sight without arousing their suspicion while I retrieved my timepiece and its transmitter; made my appeal to the boy.

That I would catch Fraan in it I would never have believed.

But I had. There he was, plainly and unmistakably. His antiseptic-looking face, the too-large-looking blond head tilted a little to the side as though he were listening to me and not looking directly at me, leapt out from the thinning crowd as my viewer went to its highest magnification.

I shook my head. "I don't see him," I lied. "But it was worth taking the shot on the odd chance that he might still have been there, or come back."

I hoped that the boy, if he was listening, knowing that I couldn't have missed him in my shot, would know that I was covering for him now; know and be reassured.

Plagiar wasn't being of any help to me. "It will be a nice melon for us to cut up," he said. "Fifty thousand . . ." his voice emphasizing the amount, ". . . fifty thousand Earthside dollars for the boy."

I knew he was talking not for me but for his bully boys, keeping their sights on simple money, explaining his interest in me in terms that would mask it but really were only the scratching of the surface potential.

Well, he knew the limits of the trust he could put in his people, or maybe he just didn't trust anyone to withstand so great a temptation.

At any rate, I didn't see that it was of any help toward making the boy any more willing to trust me to hear Plagiar go on about how large the price on his head was.

I didn't know whether to be heartened or discouraged by the sight of Fraan's face in the transhaus crowd.

Heartened by the thought that if he had Baas' receiver, he might have figured out my act about parking it while pretending sleep and seeing me being taken inside the transhaus, would listen for a signal.

Discouraged. He didn't have the receiver . . . and if he had, by mingling topside with the crowd, he was in a good spot not to be listening to it.

There was no help for it. I had to repeat my call and keep repeating it as often as I dared . . . and the risk of getting caught at it was just one more thing for me to keep pushed to the back of my mind and out of my thinking.

I coughed. I coughed heavily and, I hoped, convincingly, groping with one hand in my pockets for the packet of tissues I knew I did not have.

My other hand I held over my mouth, mumbling, gasping my apologies even as I pretended to be strangling on my own breath. Catching it in my throat and straining, feeling my eyeballs bulge and water.

Hort, the bully boy I'd gifted with his aching throat, watched me with obvious satisfaction for a long moment after Plagiar had waved to him to hand me a drink.

I took it from him. "Tissues," I wheezed. "Do you have a packet of tissues?"

My gasp was one of relief mingled with satisfaction when Brigit fished one out of her shoulder purse beside her and handed it to me.

"Thank you," I said, brushing it, heavy with her scent, across my mouth, before I put it in my inside pocket.

My inside pocket, the one which also held my wrist-chrono. I had not had it on my wrist earlier, I did not want to call attention to it by wearing it now.

I was now set, if my hands had not forgotten their long-ago skill with magic, to palm my wrist-chrono and bring it up to my mouth under cover of Brigit's packet of tissues.

Bring it up to my mouth and, from time to time, whisper into it my message to the boy.

Whisper it under the vigilant eyes of Plagiar and his bully boys who were watching me in shifts. Whisper and hope not to be caught.

Meanwhile, in the next room was a trunk.

A trunk that, if Rolf Sklar was to be believed, had been booby-trapped by a man whose specialty was not in any field that could be expected to give him a familiarity with the trickiness of explosives. A man who, moreover, had rigged his trap while undergoing a mental turmoil that pressed him close to the border of sanity.

A bomb devised and set by a man of no experience and teetering on the brink.

I moved my tongue in my cotton-dry mouth, and when I coughed and asked the bully boy for a second drink, my voice came rasping from my throat with a hoarseness that was all its own and none of my doing.

Chapter Twenty-six

Outside the windows of Plagiar's suite the moonless Poldrogi night was closing in. I saw the reflected glare of the crime-lights begin its paced march to full intensity and again forced back the unthinking animal urge to openly break and run.

There was another way to be tried first, and the time for it had at long last come.

I stretched in my chair, made a great show of flexing my cramped neck, arms, shoulders.

The two bully boys Plagiar had left with me were at the alert at once.

I blinked at them. "I don't know about you," I said, "but the clock inside my head tells me I ought to be asleep. Will one of you call the transhaus for me and see if they're cleaned up enough to let me back in to hit the sack?"

I had expected them to laugh and to tell me that I was going exactly nowhere. Instead, one of them got up and walked to the communicator on Plagiar's table.

He pressed down a tab, spoke into the unit and, in a moment, turned back to me. "Come," he said. "We will take you."

I had all I could do to keep from staring at him. My plan had been unimaginative but, I hoped, workable. I'd expected a lengthy harangue at the end of which I hoped to get acoss the idea that, if they meant to keep me here, the least they could do was to let me get my gear. Gear that I had to collect personally because it was my thumb alone that would open the lock of the transhaus safebox in which I'd left it.

Some time, somewhere, during that escorted trip I hoped to lose my jailers, in a way as yet unformed in my thinking, hinging on what chance would hand me.

Once away, I meant to make straight for the one place I hoped they would not seek to find me, the one place I'd been telling them right along I was headed for. The transhaus.

But here were the bully boys, one of them shrugging his meaty shoulders to settle his blue and yellow tunic, holding open the door for me.

I got a second charge when we reached the parking area level and stepped from the elevator, the bully boys half a step behind me.

A blatting sound, more of a snarl. Twice, in such rapid succession that I could not be sure of the direction from which it came.

Behind me the bully boys went down. Silently, without so much as a grunt from either to signal that they'd each taken the jolt of a stun gun.

My body's reflex had dropped me into a crouch. Peering around, not knowing where to look in the shadow-casting harsh overhead lights for whoever it was that had fired on us, I could not know if the blast had been meant for me and gotten the bully boys when it went off target, or if the aim had been true and hit its intended mark.

A movement at the foot of the spiral fire ramp caught at me and I spun around to face it.

I knew her almost before she stepped out from behind the shield of an upright column. Brigit. I could only stare at the weapon she held level in her hand.

"Hurry," she said, dropping it into her purse hung from its strap over her shoulder, "before someone comes."

She gestured in the direction, not of her small two-seated skimmer, but of the heavier, much faster black and white vehicle I'd seen the bully boys riding in earlier.

My gasp of relief at seeing her put her blaster away was sincere and loud to the point of embarrassment, but still I hung back.

"Whose side are you on?" I wanted to know and was rewarded by an impatient look from Brigit.

"Do not be stupid," she said. "Just how large a share do you think Anton has in mind to give me?"

"And you think I'll be more generous?" I said.

"Since you seem determined to move as swiftly as a stone," she said, "I will put it bluntly. I think you will be easier to cheat. Now get in ... and hurry."

I clambered into the skimmer beside her, laughing, at what I wasn't sure. Or maybe it was just a senseless reaction to the tension I'd been under these past hours; felt no release from even now.

I needed no more than a microsecond to weigh her sincerity. I knew the effort to be useless.

Brigit fired up the skimmer, looking at me, dark

eyebrows up and arched, even as she leaned forward to do so.

I answered her unspoken "Where to?"

"The transhaus," I said, and, for no reason at all, thought of the red mark on her fingertip Brigit had been examining as the bully boys had thrust me into Anton Plagiar's presence, after they'd caught me crouched, with her, behind a row of parked skimmers.

The skimmer lifted up, a little heavily I thought, and Brigit started to ease it out of its parking spot ... and I got my largest charge of all.

Near the top of the ramp, leaning back against the wall, lax as only the young can be, I saw a figure.

He wore stained coveralls and his face was streaked with patches of masking grease, but even at this distance I knew him. Knew him as instantly as I'd known Brigit.

Fraan. The boy Plagiar hunted ... and he was here and not beside my bunk at the transhaus for which I was about to head.

I was startled. So startled that I had not the wit or the time to hide my astonishment.

But then I caught myself. Why shouldn't he be here? I didn't know the range of the pickup on the transmitter in my wrist-chrono, but it was plain now that the boy had been hearing everything I'd heard or said for close to a dozen hours.

It was also plain that he must be aware, by now, that I was the only one who could identify him on sight. It struck me to wonder if he was here to make our getting together easier, or to safeguard at least the visual aspects of his identity by eliminating me.

My sudden start had not escaped Brigit. "What?" she said, and she was peering up toward the head of the ramp. "What is it? What did you see?"

"Nothing," I said. "Nothing at all."

But the boy was erect now and he was not to be missed.

"I see him," she said, her voice suddenly tight and excited. "It is the boy, isn't it?"

My scar was itching, but the impulse in me was strong. Brigit, by blasting my bully boy escort, had thrown her lot in with mine. She'd also made it impossible for me to deny Fraan's identity and return to Plagiar's suite to wait for another chance to meet with the boy.

It was now, or Lord knew when ... if ever.

"Yes," I said. "Slow it down. Stop. Pick him up."

But Fraan was moving, running lightly into the street.

Beside me Brigit was shouting. "It is the boy! He is getting away ... stop him ... stop him ... !"

Behind me I sensed motion and when I turned to look I saw Hort, a stun gun in his left hand, thrusting up and forward from the floor of the skimmer's back seat. Dvar was already partway out of the open window on his side, his stun gun emerging from its holster in the singleness of his motion. And I knew why the skimmer had seemed to me to rise heavily at its starting.

The boy was on my side of the skimmer and it was Hort's misfortune that he was, too.

"Run," I shouted. "Run, Fraan, it's a trap."

And even as I was straining my lungs, I was turning in my seat. It was the awkwardest of positions, and I felt in my shoulder a sharp hot sting of stretching tendons as I reached back and out with my arm.

I had no leverage, I had no strength, but with my outstretched fingers I could slap.

And slap I did, across Hort's eyes.

It was a puny blow, as such, but it was effective ... and it was the last thing he could take coming from me.

He fell back against the seat, both hands up, their backs digging and rubbing at his eyes.

The backs of his hands, because the fingers of one were splinted and rigid, the others gripped his stun gun.

His gun hand came down. Came down enough for me to see the red eye, streaming tears and glaring. The teeth bared in a grimace of fury.

Down came the stun gun, inches.

Inches only until it pointed full into my face.

I saw it coming, and I tried to duck away, but my arm over the back of my seat, my body twisted, held me back.

Dvar, the other bully boy, struck down on Hort's arm, but the gun went off all the same.

At this close range, even the cushioning of the seat back could not save me entirely.

I felt the numbness strike and my body begin its limp, helpless, slumping down.

I'd been told that to be hit by a stun-gun jolt was not particularly painful ... but that man had either never been hit or was a liar.

I was numb, all right, but I also ached all over. Ached with the constricted intensity of a pain that felt as though it should have been throbbing, but wasn't ... couldn't.

I almost welcomed the blackness that was nudging itself mushily into my brain, even though its coming meant I would not know if my distracting swipe at Hort had given Fraan the extra split-moment he needed to make good his escape.

Chapter Twenty-seven

Tingles.
Tingles. Tiny, sharp, aching, like those of a leg that has fallen asleep and is now coming awake.
But this leg is all up and down my body, both sides, my arms out to my fingertips.
My scalp. Even in my scalp I feel the tiny needles jabbing, prickling.
I tried to move my head and the swelling surge of needles brought streaks of red to bursting at the lining back of my eyeballs.
Red. Red in my eyes and Brigit's face peering down at me.
Brigit examining a red mark on her fingertip.
A red mark like a tiny half moon ... on her fingertip ... and the bully boys shoving me into a room.
And even my fuzzing brain knew the answer to that.
Brigit, crouched down behind a skimmer, her arm up to the partition close behind her, her finger pressing hard on a button.
A button that was there to summon the parking area attendant from wherever he might be ... a

button that would leave its half-moon mark on her finger from the hardness of her pressing.

It had been no accident, then, that I had been come upon from behind by the attendant with a stun gun in his hand ... come upon and delivered to Plagiar's laughing bully boys.

And if it was Brigit who'd betrayed me then, was it Brigit who'd betrayed me now?"

"Lied," I said, and my tongue was thick and it tingled as I forced it to move. "Lied, you lied to me."

The face peering down into mine smiled. "I asked what you thought my share would be and then I told you that you would be easy to cheat ... where did I lie?"

"Lies," I said. "Lies," and it was floating out of my mind why my tongue should be saying that word of itself.

I heard a man laughing. "A little more time. They all come out of it feeling put upon."

Put upon....

I had been masher-beam grazed, riot-dyed, judo-chopped ... and now stun-blasted.

I had been lied to, chased by a lynch mob, and sucked into the treasure hunt of the ages for a reason I still did not know.

I was suspected in two killings and would be in a third if Rook's trunk was ever opened without it blasting away a city acre.

Put upon. Some ape was laughing because I was coming awake feeling put upon.

"He is grating his teeth," I heard Brigit say.

"That is normal," said the man's voice and now I knew it to be that of Anton Plagiar. "It has something to do with the body storing up its frustrations during the time it cannot move freely, I suspect."

I *was* grating my teeth. Now I deliberately forced the knots at the sides of my jaws to loosen, tried to let my body fall limp and loose so that perhaps the ache and the tingling would ease.

"Get him up on his feet," I heard Plagiar say. "Walk him around, I don't want discoloration to form."

I felt hands tugging at me, lifting me up, and there was nothing I could do except go with them.

Discoloration. The same man who'd said a stunbolt didn't hurt had also said that exercise, begun as soon as possible after control is regained and kept up until the breathing is heavy and the heart pounding, would help prevent an aftereffect that otherwise left the body looking bruised over its entire surface.

He'd been a liar about the pain, he could be a liar about this. I wanted down ... sit ... lie down ... anything to ease the crescendo of needles I felt at each movement the hands gripping me forced me to go through.

"He is sweating," someone said.

"Good," said Plagiar's voice. "He is over the worst of it."

And with the first outpouring of sweat I realized that even in Poldrogi's heat, my skin, up to this moment, had been dry and powdered feeling.

"I'm all right," I said, and now I could feel that the hands gripping me had to use their strength to keep me from jerking myself free to stand glaring at Plagiar and the others in the room.

The others. Brigit. Dvar. Hort. The two bully boys Brigit had blasted.

The two bully boys Brigit had blasted!

The two of them standing there, grinning at me. Neither of them looking in the least as though they'd just gotten over what I was going through.

They caught the wide-mouthed gape I could not yet control and their grins grew broader. Plagiar laughed. "Surely you did not think that Brigit actually blasted my men, did you?"

I closed my mouth. "No," I mumbled. "No, I suppose not."

It was beginning to soak into my addled brain that Plagiar was not being solicitous of my welfare when he'd ordered his men to keep the bruise effect from forming on my body. A man who wished to avoid police attention enough to have his bodyguards use riot weapons in subduing a possible assassin, as had the men who'd dye-stained me on the platform, would also not want stun-bruises to be in evidence to spark questions.

And Plagiar didn't need me now that Brigit and two ... maybe four ... of his bully boys had seen Fraan.

Now that my head was clearing I sensed about Plagiar, about Brigit, an air of waiting. Even Dvar and Hort seemed to have it.

I felt a surge of hope. A hope that the boy, with his masking of grease and coveralls, was not recognizable, had made it safely out of sight and away.

Plagiar chilled the hope almost at once. A pocket communicator on his table sounded lightly and he lifted up a tiny earpiece before he flipped a tab.

He nodded. "Fine," he said. "Cautiously now. We do not want to startle him into running again. And do not let your taking of him be seen, do you understand?"

He said, "Fine," several times more before he flipped the tab off again and put down his earpiece.

He did not have to spell it out for me. He could not very well have his men pounce upon their victim and wrestle him to the ground. Not in the full glare of the city's crime-lights, not on a strange world where, however influential Plagiar might be, he and his people were at best but visitors.

They did not need to openly wrestle anyone. Not if they were Plagiar's men and practiced in unobtrusive action.

The boy was still at large, but if I was reading the look on Plagiar's face aright, it was now only a matter of scant minutes.

So few that even now Brigit was beckoning to Hort to follow her and I knew that when they came back into the room they would be wheeling Rook's disguised trunk before them.

I had a hope left, a double one, hinging on the transmitter hidden in my wrist-chrono in my pocket.

The boy, from what Plagiar had said into his communicator, was not running now. Might even think that he had lost his pursuers. If I could but bring my timepiece up to my mouth and speak into it secretly again, I might still warn him of his imminent capture ... might still help him evade it.

The police corporal had told me that his people had broken the scrambled signal the transmitter was sending and that he would be monitoring it. If while warning Fraan, I could at the same time summon him, his police might arrive in time to catch Plagiar with Rook's trunk ... and his dead body ... or at least get here in time to save my neck from whatever Plagiar had planned for it once he was sure he had the boy.

The pressure of Brigit's packet of tissues was light in my pocket and I coughed and started to reach for it.

I coughed and I started to reach, but stopped in mid-motion.

A grinning Plagiar was dangling from his finger, pulled at that moment from its concealment in the pile of papers on his table in front of him, my wrist-chrono.

My mouth was suddenly raspingly dry.

"When?" I croaked, "when ... did ... you ... ?"

"When did I first suspect what it was you were doing ... or when did I take your chrono from you?"

"When?" I said, and though I was making the effort, I could make my voice no stronger, no clearer.

"I took it from you when you were unconscious, of course."

He laughed. "I suspected what you were doing when I noticed a certain arching to your hand when you had it up to your face."

He let my timepiece drop back onto the table, his eyes looking vastly amused, his manner expansive.

Expansive. I supposed I would feel expansive, too, if I thought I at long last had in my grasp what Plagiar thought he was about to have in his ... or I knew the person to whom I was talking would not get to repeat what he was hearing.

Plagiar. "... the palming of an object does have about it a look recognizable to the knowing eye. Surely, Pike, as one dabbler in magic to another, you did not really have more than a forlorn hope that your little subterfuge would go undetected."

I did not answer him. I could not answer him. He had seen what I was about and he had used it, and me, to bring him the key he needed to realize his fortune.

The fortune the true proportions of which he did not trust his men to know and, knowing, retain their loyalty to him . . . perhaps even to keep their sanity.

. . . knowing, to keep their sanity. . . ?

Plagiar knew the true potential.

Brigit knew the true potential.

And I knew.

From a drawer in his table Anton Plagiar was taking a flat, oddly shaped handgun; one with the double-barreled look of a slim, pencil-sized tube projecting from inside a larger, stumpier one.

A laser weapon . . . the kind that had killed Mahar Baas.

My hope for the boy's escape was gone. For myself there was suddenly the racing of my heart and the breathy, top-of-the-lungs feel of naked danger.

Chapter Twenty-eight

They came back into the room wheeling the trunk in its taboret disguise; Hort pushing it, Brigit close behind him.

Plagiar sat at his table, his laser pistol, the safety off, lying at the ready in front of him ... and I knew what he was saving me for.

The trunk. Not even Dvar and Hort, the men who had stolen it for him from Sklar, knew fully what it contained. When the boy who was to key it was brought in and the time came for it to be opened, I was sure that Plagiar meant to have in the room only the people who shared its secret with him.

Brigit ... and myself.

I did not need to wonder to whom Plagiar intended to delegate the not-pleasant-to-think-about task of actually breaking open its closed sides.

"How long," I said, intending to ask how long Rook's body had been in it, but instead I said, "how long have you been hunting the boy?"

"Months," Plagiar said. "Months."

His avid stare was centered on the trunk, leaving

me to comtemplate for myself what would hit me when, under his gun, I would shove open the trunk and bring into the light its secret ... leaving me to contemplate the thought that, afterward, there would be no appreciably greater difficulty getting rid of the stripped trunk if, in addition to Rook's, it held a second body.

Mine.

The trunk sat on a wheeled base, its sides draped with a magic symbol emblazoned hanging. The coin-sized disk that I'd felt rub my thumb was set down into its top. The whole looked credibly like what it was intended to look like, a magician's taboret.

Plagiar's laser pistol, the safety off, was very prominent in my eyes.

"All right," he said, using his left hand to gesture at the two bully boys whom Brigit had pretended to blast in the parking area below. "Dvar and Hort can handle it, you two go."

And when the two men were gone, he spoke to Hort. "Strip it," he said, indicating the trunk. "Remove that magic nonsense."

Perhaps I was jumpy, my nerves stretched taut to the point where I could almost hear their twang inside my head, but I had the feeling that Hort hesitated before he walked to the taboret and started to rip away at the hangings.

"The top," Plagiar said, "lift off the top and the rest will come with it."

Hort had ripped the hangings up the front and now he tilted the top up and back and slid it somewhat awkwardly to the back of the trunk top.

I could now see that the disk was flush with the

trunk surface and completely separated from the false top Hort had just taken away.

"The card production," I said, "it has no connection with the disk at all."

Plagiar laughed. "How could it?" And then to Hort, "Bring it here."

But Hort had already thrust a finger of his uninjured hand through the hole in the taboret top which he had not lifted away completely, but kept standing on edge, the draping cover still covering a side of the trunk.

In a moment, the slender wand with the card on its tip popped out. It was still the trey of diamonds.

"A completely separate arrangement," Plagiar said, "It enabled me to keep the real device available at an instant's notice."

He sounded and looked satisfied to the point of smugness.

His communicator startled me with its sounding. Instantly Plagiar was at it, the earpiece to his ear. When he put it down, I did not need to hear the words to know what he was about to say.

"They have the boy. They are on the way."

And if he had been on his feet I was sure that he would have danced a jig. As it was, he leaned back and rubbed his palms together.

Rubbed his palms together, his head thrown back, his breathing heavy.

The pistol in front of him. Leap for it now?

And then I saw the turn of Hort's head to look at Brigit, saw her nod, saw the fat-barreled, carbine-length weapon come up from its hiding place in the taboret hangings Hort had handled so awkwardly.

I heard its masher beam whir once ... in the direction of Plagiar. And then Hort had snapped it to his right, fired again, and was back to cover Plagiar.

I heard the dead fall of the body and I did not have to look to know that Dvar's brain could literally not have had the time to know what hit it.

Plagiar had snatched up his pistol and was firing it at Hort.

At least his hand was moving in that curious pumping action of a man pulling a trigger again and again ... but nothing was happening except that as his hand pumped he seemed to be having trouble keeping his arm up; staying in his seat.

The masher beam. Its peripheral shock wave had struck him and now his nerves were feeling the same shock effect as had mine when I'd been hit on his dipping and pitching stage platform.

Hort stood his ground behind the trunk, his sniper's carbine pointing easily at Plagiar, snaking between him and me ... and I knew who it was who'd fired the shot at me at the Wayfarer's Home.

Who it was that had been beside Brigit on the roof, dropped down out of sight behind the parapet, not betrayed by her not because she did not want me, hiding in the bushes, to know of him, but because she really had intended for me to kill Anton with the laser in my camera ... and be dropped myself in the next instant by Hort. It was Anton who must not know of Hort.

Seeing me bring my camera up to the ready she could think only that I was taking the Anton-double to be the real man and meant to shoot without waiting for her signal.

She had tried to stop me with her frantic waving, not knowing it was only the habit of my hands, checking my camera for the strangeness of its feel, that had triggered the killer laser prematurely.

The killer laser that Hort had slipped into it in the brief moment it had been out of my hands, sitting beside Brigit's purse on the bench outside the Home study.

I knew all these things in an instant, the instant it took Brigit to nod to Hort and for him to fire his weapon.

Did I also know who, guarding Brigit during her meeting with me in the blackness hard by the Wayfarer's Home, a meeting he had helped arrange by slipping me her note, had bashed in Rolf Sklar's head when he came upon him moving up on us in the dark?

It was Brigit who spoke. "You might live a little longer, Anton, if you will sit back and stop trying to fire that silly pistol of yours. It will not work."

That was true. It wouldn't. Hort had fired his carbine, not at Plagiar, but at the pistol on his table. A near miss would have been enough. Its emiting crystal was fairly sturdy and might survive, but the envelopes of its twinned light-source tubes were wine glass thin and could not, and had not, withstood the vibration of even the beam's brushing touch.

Anton clutched at the edge of his table, fighting to stay upright, and I wondered if when I was hit my face had been as sick-looking as his was now.

But I did not dwell on the thought. Hort's carbine, snaking between me and Plagiar, suddenly came to rest on me alone.

"Do we need him?" he said over his shoulder to Brigit.

She laughed. "We don't if you do not mind opening the trunk yourself when the boy gets here."

She indicated the trembling Plagiar with a tilt of her head. "Anton will be no help."

Hort studied me for a long moment before he shot a glance at the trunk.

"I think I know what you mean," he said, and he laughed.

It wasn't until I let it out in a noisy gasp that I realized I'd been holding my breath.

Holding my breath and trying hard not to see the broken fingers I'd given Hort, the face patches ... trying hard not to think of my chop across his throat ... of the slap across his eyes.

Trying hard and not making it.

Chapter Twenty-nine

Plagiar had made it over to the larger of the room's two sofas on his own. Neither Brigit nor Hort had done more than watch him make the trip on sagging legs. I knew something of what he was going through, but I'm not sure I would have helped him even if I hadn't had Hort's weapon to keep me from moving from where I was.

Plagiar sat back in one corner, his feet up and crossed, his arms tight against his chest and stomach. From the look of his face I judged that he was getting as used to the ebb and flow of his strength, the phasing feeling of it, as I had when Hort's sniper beam had whirred past me.

"You want it all ... and you want me dead," Plagiar said, and he sounded as though he could not believe what he was saying.

Brigit did not bother to smile. "I take from you no more than you tried to take from Rolf Sklar," she said. "If you had not leapt upon him at once and taken his trunk, he would have had Baas come back with the boy from wherever they were hiding and all would have been well. He would not have had a reason to approach me, to persuade me to join forces with him so that between us we could cope with what he could not handle alone ... your greed."

Persuade her. I wondered just how hard a job Sklar had had doing that ... and would he be alive now if he hadn't succeeded?

"You want me dead," Plagiar said again, still sounding as though he couldn't believe his words.

He raised his eyes to me. "Then you were working for her and not on behalf of the boy when you tried to kill me with the weapon in your camera."

So that was why he had covered for me with the police, removing the laser, restoring my camera. Thinking that, working for the boy, if I were not free I could not lead him to his quarry.

Well, in spite of my ignorance of what I was in the middle of, I had.

I looked at Brigit. "Why me?" I said, remembering what, riding in her skimmer, she had told me of how she had come to hire me at the transhaus. "Sklar didn't give you my name ... tell you where to find me. He couldn't have."

The puzzlement in her eyes looked genuine. "But he did," she said. "At first, when he told me you were an innocent he had found for us to sacifice so that we could dispose of Anton with no risk to ourselves, I believed him. But then when I saw him offering you all the money he had, I knew he'd lied to me ... that you really were working with Baas and knew where the boy was. That he'd found you and was hoping, through me, to get rid of two obstacles—you and Anton—at the same time."

Not *all* his money, I said to myself, remembering the discrepancy in the numbers that were supposed to have been on the sight-draft he'd pushed toward me at the gasthaus, and what the police corporal said he'd withdrawn. Not all his money.

I wondered if Sklar really thought I was with Baas and had tried to kill me as Brigit had just suggested ... or did he come to me in full sight of all to drag me like a red herring across some unknown trail of his own?

"You are a false woman," Plagiar said to Brigit. He looked up at Hort, standing over him, his carbine held loosely in the crook of his arm. "Do not trust her as I did," he said. "She will get to you when she is ready. She wants it all."

Hort grinned down at him. "You cannot get me at her throat," he said. "We will not fall out." And he nudged the fallen body of Dvar with his toe. "She knows that if I hang, she hangs with me. It is as simple as that."

Brigit might have been joking, but she sounded genuinely hurt. "Hort," she said, "you wouldn't."

He spread his grin to include her in it along with Plagiar. "Do not put me to the test, loved one. Do not put me to the test."

The communicator on Plagiar's table sounded and I saw the color suddenly flush high in Brigit's cheeks and a hard glitter come into her eyes.

She reached over Plagiar to take the carbine from Hort's hand, prodded Plagiar with it.

"Answer them," she said. "Answer them and tell them Hort will be down for the boy. Tell them to return to their stations, that you will need them no more tonight. And Anton ... do not be stupid and try to say more."

She stood over Plagiar, the carbine pressed against his skull as he spoke. And when he was through she stepped back and motioned him away from the communicator and back to his seat on the sofa.

Her finger was inside the trigger guard of the carbine, its barrel upright now, the curved butt resting on one hip. She handled the weapon with a practiced ease that killed any thought I might have had of wresting it from her grip once Hort was out of the room.

The sight of Plagiar's pistol, lying on the tabletop where he'd let it fall from his phasing fingers, was made doubly galling for me by my knowing that it would not fire.

"Bring the boy up," she said to Hort. "And be sure that you return alone."

"They will not know," Hort said. "They will not suspect." And he was gone, leaving me under Brigit's watchful eyes and the unnatural glitter that was strong in them.

The silence swelled until all I could hear to break it was the heavy rasping that was the sound of my own breathing; the low retch that was Plagiar at the turning of a phase, and now ... as I strained to hear Hort returning with the boy ... a faintly blubbering sound that I did not place until I saw that it was keeping pace with the rise and fall of Brigit's breathing through her parted lips.

Chapter Thirty

Sounds.

Sounds of the elevator opening and closing.

Footsteps.

Sounds of doors being opened and closed, of locks being snapped shut again.

Sounds to raise the strain of listening to Brigit's breathing grow tighter, see the quiver of the carbine's upraised tip increase, the glitter of her eyes grow glassy.

Then Hort was back in the room, thrusting the boy in before him.

The boy who moved easily, unresistingly, in his stained coveralls, and who did not lose his balance at Hort's hard shove.

The boy who stood as erect as I remembered him to have in the transhaus corridor when he'd led us to the body of Mahar Baas.

Erect, and on his face a calm that even the streaks of grease with which he'd tried to mask himself could not completely hide.

"I'm sorry, Fraan," I said. "I did not mean for you to be caught."

His eyes, moving toward me, and his voice were as calm as his face. Oddly so.

"You are a friend," he said, and to me he sounded as though he was saying it more to identify me for himself than as if he meant it to be a comfort to me.

The upraised tip of the carbine was shaking visibly and I felt a kind of relief when Brigit handed the weapon back to Hort.

"Watch them," she said, and she took hold of the boy's wrist.

He did not move, and she tugged at his arm. "Come," she said, and again, "come."

Hort prodded him with the tip of the carbine and the boy looked at it and at him with no change of expression that I could see.

But he moved.

He moved to the side of the trunk and let Brigit lift up his hand to the disk set into its top.

Laughter. Retching, weak laughter, but laughter.

I swung on Plagiar. So did Hort with his carbine.

Brigit stopped in mid-motion, the boy's finger extended in the grip of her hand, the tip of it pointed toward the disk on the trunk, not yet touching.

Plagiar laughing. "It would be funny," he gasped, with his weakening-phase lungs. "It would be oh so funny if Pike has led us to the wrong boy."

"You are a fool," Brigit spat at him. "You checked his fingerprint yourself."

And she thrust Fraan's hand down the remaining scant inch it had been held hovering over the disk.

She thrust it down almost viciously and she held it down.

Nothing.

Nothing happened.

No whine of equipment activating, no click of a holding latch snapping back.

Nothing.

The thought of grease from his coveralls or his face coating his finger occurred to her as it occurred to me.

She jerked Fraan's finger up from the disk, wiped it angrily with her skirt, the blubbering sound of her breathing growing loud enough now for me to hear it without straining.

Back to the disk she moved the boy's hand, he all the while watching her do so with as much interest as might be displayed by a huge doll.

Shock, I thought to myself. The boy is in a state of shock that borders on the catatonic.

Now Brigit had his finger back to the disk, pressing it down until it bent back at the joint of its tip, her own growing white with the force of her gripping.

And still nothing.

She fell back, bewilderment on her face, and the boy stayed as he had been put, his finger still on the disk.

And now Brigit came forward to stare into his face, the blubbering a heave, her eyes almost on stalks with the intensity of her looking.

And she screamed.

She screamed a scream of raw rage that opened her mouth wide and brought flecks of foam to its corners.

She screamed and she clawed at the boy's eyes.

She clawed and even Hort took a step forward before he saw what she was about.

She clawed, but only at the boy's left eye, at the

eyebrow above it; he not bringing up an arm to stop her.

She clawed and I felt the start of a shudder as I saw the skin come away in a clinging strip.

But it was only the start of a shudder that stopped when I realized I saw no blood; saw only the faintly lilac-glowing "A."

An android!

Fraan was an android! Of course he couldn't activate a cell-keyed lock. Of course he would have the real Fraan's fingerprints.

He would have the fingerprints of anybody you chose to make a cast of for a pattern. It was evident that Baas had managed the time for at least that much before he ran.

I laughed. Laughed without being able to help it. Laughed because I suddenly remembered something that the police corporal had told me about Baas.

That when he disappeared from his university's lab there had vanished with him equipment that his employers did not wish to talk about.

A bio lab ... a bioelectronic device ... an android. And, of course, they would not wish such laxness in their security to be known, at least not until that valuable property was safely back under wraps again.

Mahar Baas.

Mahar Baas was not the blackmailer coming to him for what he could get that Rolf Sklar had taken him to be; a tool to be used to keep key and trunk apart until Plagiar could be contained or killed.

Mahar Baas was, instead, the friend of August Rook who realized that he had been duped into helping another steal the fruits of Rook's work.

The friend who perhaps sought to recover those fruits for Rook's son ... or at least to confirm his suspicions as to Rook's fate ... but whom Sklar alerted to the real danger when he spoke to him of Plagiar and the need for getting the boy safely out of reach.

The friend who stole from the bio lab in which he worked with the boy's father a piece of highly sophisticated equipment, the android he needed to be the wild goose in the chase he meant to lead them all.

His trail, hiding it enough to keep his pursuers unsuspecting, yet open enough for them to follow him while he led them away from their real prey.

Acting exactly as Sklar had told him to, except in one respect, in one all-important respect.

Brigit caught the thought as quickly as I did.

"Baas!" she shrieked. "Baas! He never took him away at all. The boy is still with his mother."

Hort. He was goggling at Brigit, the masher-beam carbine sagging.

Now. Leap upon him now!

But even as I started my move, Hort caught it and for me to complete it meant only to throw myself directly into the beam of the carbine coming up.

But I had started to move. I could not stop now. I could only change direction.

To the side I went. To the side and over the top of Plagiar's table, tipping it over with me.

Over and down, in a flurry of flying papers, of crashing sound, of a sliding, wrecked pistol, to crouch behind the puny shelter of the overturned top.

"Kill him." Brigit shrieked. "Kill him. Kill him."

"Gladly," I heard Hort say. "But not with this. Not quickly. Not easily. I owe him too much to do him that favor."

I spun around to dart a quick look over the top of the table edge before I dropped down again.

Hort had handed his carbine to Brigit and my quick glimpse had shown me him beginning to remove his blue and yellow tunic. It was plain he meant to pay me back for the broken fingers, the mashed face, the simple indignity of his having to take the punishment from me.

And beyond him was the wild-eyed Brigit with the carbine poised.

I pounded the floor with my fist, danger and frustration choking me ... and then I saw Plagiar's pistol ... and at the same time felt the flail of my record camera in the sleeve pocket of my jumpsuit.

I snatched up the wrecked pistol, pressed on its hooded top, struggling for a breath-stopping moment with its refusal to budge.

The masher beam, if its vibration had disturbed the molecules of the metal, of what use... ?

The top snapped open and the gun almost flew out of my hands with the sudden release.

I caught at it, peered inside, swearing at the sweat expressing its desire to have me killed by pouring down into my eyes at just that moment.

I peered and I saw that I was right. The long crystal that emitted the invisible rays that made of this laser a killing weapon was intact, but the bits of broken glass demonstrated that the tubes that were the source of exciting light had indeed not withstood the vibration's touch. Their tiny foil reflectors sagged at my touch.

I put the pistol on the floor and snatched at my sleeve pocket and my record camera in it.

The windows in front of the flashtubes that provided the light for its pictures gave me no trouble. No trouble at all, and I threw them aside and reached for the tiny flashtubes they were meant to protect.

"You, behind there. Pike. Do you hear me?"

It was Hort, ready for me now, ready and limbering, and having his fun making me sweat.

Well, sweating I was. Sweating, my fingers slippery with it. Fingers slippery and the glass surface of the tiny flashtube at which they probed slick.

Ah, I had it free of its clip.

And now I had its mate as well.

The pistol.

Could I fit them to the pistol?

Short. They are too short to reach from terminal to terminal. Only a little, but too short.

"Pike. Come out. I promise to kick you only when you are down."

He was laughing. Moving in toward the table behind which I crouched. My back was against the upright panel of its top, my hands were feverishly busy with Plagiar's wrecked pistol.

Closer, moving leisurely, but coming closer.

Clips. Bend the pistol's clips to reach.

How?

Don't have the leverage with my fingers alone . . . have no tool.

Foil. Foil reflectors can conduct current. Slide them. Press them down and slide them a little to make them reach.

No. Metal too light. Will not stand the current. Blow out with first shot.

Nothing else. Hort close upon you.
Nothing else.
Hold. May not need but one shot.
One shot.

All it takes is but one shot to prove a gun works.

I slid the tiny foil scraps endwise, creasing them to make contacts for my flashtubes with the pistol's clips. I slammed shut the hooded top, came up over the edge of the table with the pistol in my hand and pointing.

Pointing.

Even a pistol that you know does not work, pointed dead at you will give you pause, stop you in your tracks, if only for a moment.

Hort stopped.

Then he laughed and moved forward again and I pulled the pistol's trigger.

I fired it.

I fired Plagiar's jury-rigged wreck of a pistol.

I fired it, but not at Hort.

I fired it at Brigit.

Brigit who on the rim of my vision I saw bringing her masher carbine to a line on me.

Brigit who dropped the weapon and spun back, clutching at her side.

The left. The vibration has shifted the lenses to throw to the left.

Hort was frozen in his tracks, staring not at me, but at the weapon he had thought to be dead now come to life in my hand.

I kept him that way.

Kept him frozen in his tracks with it and at the same time spoke to Plagiar.

To Plagiar who, sitting back in the corner of his sofa, had about him an air of holding back that I knew from my own experience meant he was waiting for a stronger point in the phasing of his strength to leap for the carbine lying on the floor.

"Don't you try it," I said. And inched over until I could feel it under my hand.

Only after I had picked up the fallen weapon did I let my gaze lessen its darting between Plagiar, sullen in his corner, and Hort, now recovered and watching me.

And Brigit. Eyes hot with anger and pain. Holding her side, sagged back against the floor where her seared side had dropped her.

"Back," I said to Hort, making the motion with the carbine. "Back."

And when he was clear of the tipped table I sidled toward it sideways and hooked the cord of the fallen communicator with one foot.

I did not duck down behind the table, nor did I take my eyes from the three in front of me.

I pulled on the cord with my foot until the communicator was out in sight. Then I squatted down beside it, pressed the tab carrying the hostel's own symbol and, when the genteel voice answered, asked for the police.

He was a good hostel man. He would have stalled until his own security people could come up and have a try at keeping any matter calling for police attention quiet.

I cut him short. "The city police. A corporal, bald head, never got his name. Anyone else who comes through the door gets a masher-beam bolt in the stomach."

"Yessir," he said hurriedly. "Yessir, the city police ... bald corporal," And I could hear the sound of his fumbling with the connections.

I turned to the android. "Fraan," I said, "can you hold this weapon on these people for me?"

I was afraid I knew the answer, but I had to ask the question. There was something I needed to do before the police got here.

Androids do only what they are programmed to do, so the one I'd called Fraan did not shake his head.

"No," it simply said. "I am programmed only for evasion and the leaving of a trail."

And the answer told me that, while the first explosion Brigit had told me of might have been set off by Baas, the second was the work of the android, following a preset plan that had successfully covered their escape before.

But with Baas dead, there was no one to give it new instructions to fit the new circumstances, so that it must extrapolate for itself from new material presented to it but always within the framework of its old programming.

And the new material had come to it chiefly from what it heard ... and much of that had come from the transmitter Baas had planted on me.

Well, there was no time for me to change that now, even if I'd had the know-how, which I didn't. But Hort could walk up to the android and it would not resist his taking the carbine from its hands.

I would have to go it alone.

"You," I said to Hort. "Over to the trunk."

He stared at me but he moved to the side of the upended trunk.

I set the masher beam to its narrowest angle, stood to the side, and sliced with it.

Sliced not at the lock, but down along the hinges

on the opposite side of the trunk; sliced to the sound of gasps.

Like a keen knife the beam could cut, and it did, and the hinges fell free to the floor, first the one ... and then the other.

The back of the trunk was unsecured. It could be spread open now to pivot on its catches, its lock.

"Open it," I said to Hort. "Shove it open from the back."

"Are you insane?" he flung at me. "It is keyed to explode the moment it is tampered with. The hinges. I do not know why it has not gone off already. I will not touch it."

"No!" Brigit's gasp and Plagiar's weak shout had mingled with and been lost in the sound of Hort's protest.

"Open it," I said.

Our eyes locked. Locked and held and I was bringing up the muzzle of the carbine when I heard a smashing outside the door.

"Pike," I heard, and I recognized the voice of the corporal.

"In here," I called out, and my relief at hearing the stocky corporal's voice was mixed with my chagrin at having failed to do what I felt must be done.

"You got here more quickly than I expected," I said to the corporal when the room was swarming with his men.

"We were already on the way when we got your call," he said.

"How?" I wanted to know, thinking of my wrist-chrono emptied of its transmitter and my communication with the corporal cut.

For an answer he plucked from his ear the small,

antennaed shell of a receiver. His fingers probed my left sleeve. "Your small camera, where is it?"

And when I had retrieved it from the floor behind the overturned table, he held the receiver close to it and I heard the beginning of feedback; the unmistakable high-pitched protest of a receiver too close to its transmitter.

"When we found the packet of transmitters on Sklar, I took advantage of the opportunity to plant a second one in your camera."

The corporal smiled. "I did not mention it at the time for fear that knowing of it might inhibit you."

His smile broadened, his sitting duck had led him to the killer of Baas.

Sklar.

It had to be Sklar.

Sklar, feeling secure that Baas was keeping Plagiar and the trunk and the boy away from each other, coming to Baas for a pigeon.

Sklar, who knew Rook's son and who would know the instant he laid eyes on the android how Baas had tricked him.

Know and be furious ... and in that rage kill as he had killed in rage before.

Then, his anger spent, he'd realize that Baas had made it possible for his plan to work all the better. That now he alone knew that the boy was still back at the start of the trail.

That he need only find another decoy to send Plagiar after while he, Sklar, backtracked. And that decoy he knew he had when his and Brigit's plan to have me kill Plagiar missed.

A decoy who needed only a little play-acting on Sklar's part to become colored with the appearance of authenticity.

Play-acting. Like pretending to be convinced with the others that I was Baas' accomplice and my knowledge of the boy's whereabouts might be bought with all his money ... and yet, after finding the transmitters, not wholly sure that I wasn't.

All his money drawn to prove his sincerity; only half of it offered to me because he needed the rest to run when he was ready, and he could not trust me not to pick it up and run on my own no matter how little I knew.

Play-acting to convince the others, and in the course of it and his need to be sure about me, getting his head bashed in by Hort.

I nodded at Hort, at Plagiar, at Brigit, all guarded by the corporal's men.

"What will become of them?" I asked.

The corporal shrugged. "Plagiar, I cannot say. But the one called Hort is right. They will hang together, he and the woman."

I looked at the trunk. "You know what is in the trunk?" I said to the corporal.

"Yes. I know what is in the trunk." He looked at me. "You risked knocking the hinges off. Why?"

I did not answer him, but kept looking at the trunk. "Can we open it?" I said. "Alone?"

He took a long time answering and when he finally spoke, his voice sounded as though it were coming from far away. "It can be arranged."

And when, under his direction, the room had been cleared and the prisoners moved to the anteroom, he came back in and closed the door behind him.

"I will help you," he said.

But with his hand on the trunk, he hesitated.

"Why are you so certain that it will not blow us to the sky the instant we spread its sides?"

"I never met Rook," I said. "But no matter what story he told to keep people from nosing around, I don't see a man who could worry himself half out of his mind that what he'd stumbled onto would hurt humanity, setting a trap to kill even one man, let alone whoever might be near him when he got curious about the trunk."

"You are sure of this reasoning," the corporal said.

"I would stake my life on it," I said.

"You are . . . and mine as well."

And he bent his back and we shoved open the trunk.

Epilogue

Smoke layered the air of the room in wisps and shards. Red-eyed, the corporal batted at it with his hands.

"He was one to keep many notes, this August Rook," he said.

I nodded. I had dismantled what I could of Rook's device, smashed with the butt of the carbine what I could not. Without the notes which the corporal and I had burned, it could not be recognized for what it was, let alone reconstructed.

"You are almost finished?" the corporal said.

"Yes. The disk on the trunk, I've left that where it is. It's nothing more than an adapted bio slicer, and someone may have noticed it and would ask about it if it's gone."

The corporal nodded. "It is done, then, and we will speak of this ... you and I ... to no one."

From the open window came the sound of a police vehicle approaching. The double high-low beeping of it should have sounded no different from that of any other. Yet this one had about it a certain imperiousness, a note of self-importance.

The corporal sighed audibly and redoubled his

batting at the smoke. "It is the general," he said. "This promises to be a case of much importance. Plagiar is a big man, and we have not had a quadruple killing on Poldrogi ever before. The general has a long and sensitive nose and I would not wish for the smell of burned papers to intrude itself upon his thinking."

"Don't worry," I said. "If he believes anything of what Plagiar and Brigit try to tell him, you can always fall back on there being a thermal device in the trunk that went off and burned everything the instant the vibration from my carbine hit the hinges."

But all the same I got to my feet and started helping him swat the shards of smoke toward the open window.

Heavy, Heavy

I'm six feet four, hit two hundred Earth pounds, and have a souvenir of the Second Police Action on the top of my balding head in the shape of a scar that itches when it figures I'm about to be sucked into something that, if I'm lucky, I'll live to regret.

I wish I'd paid my scar more attention when, yesterday, Keely walked up to me, put his bony hand on the padded shoulder of my slightly out-of-date travel tunic and, in that odd voice of his, invited me up to his cubicle for a friendly game to help us both while away the four days stopover time we had here on Poldrogi before the starship connection for Earthside made planetfall.

I shouldn't have needed my scar to tell me something smelled. After all, men who are as loaded as G. Warren Keely is reputed to be, don't just walk up to an ex-SpaceNav Photo Mate and invite him anywhere, much less to an intimate gaming venture of theirs.

But all I could do for now was to just sit here in the sound-conditioned quiet of Keely's room, clutching my hungry straight against the travel-worn front of my tunic and hoping that Keely, across the table from me, would not see my eyeballs popping from the strain and know I hadn't filled it.

But G. Warren Keely wasn't looking at me. His eyes in that bony face of his seemed to be staring at his cards without really taking them in and I could see the tip of his tongue flicking in and out between his thin lips. He looked tense enough to twang.

It didn't mean a thing. Keely's skinny body looked as tight-drawn as the E string on a cheap guitar whether he was holding all the aces or the well known doodle-y. And I had but two chips of my last pile left in front of me and a knot in the pit of my stomach to remind me of that hard fact.

Small as this pot was, I had a lot more riding on it than the chips and the credit disks I'd put into it. I pushed away the thought of just how much.

I licked my lips and sat, feeling the cold sweat trickling down my sides under my shirt, waiting for Keely to make up his mind.

To my left, Hale, the dealer on this hand, a stocky man with the star-and-grapple device of my own branch of the Service, SpaceNav, glowing green and delicately shaded on the back of his hand as only the Chin-Worlds can tattoo, cleared his throat.

In front of Keely a chip slipped from its balance on top of one of his piles and struck the tabletop with a tiny clatter. The sound seemed to make up his mind. I saw his eyes deep in their sockets measuring my last two chips like he was down to his last half million and wondering where his next was coming from. And then he picked up two of his own chips and dropped them onto the small pile in the center of the table.

"I'll tap you," he said, his voice tight, sounding like that of a heavily burdened fat man and not at all like what you would expect to hear coming from a dried-up looking stilt-walker like him.

I knew Keely was talking to me because Hale, and Morgan, the player on my right, had dropped out before I'd drawn the one card I hoped would fill the empty belly of my straight and missed it.

But Hale, dealing, had shoved Keely's two chips back at him with his tattooed hand. "If you have a pat hand, say so," he snapped. "Else don't be so hungry for Pike's blood before you draw."

But Hale didn't sound annoyed. Why should he be, with what had been my chips piled in front of him almost as high as in front of Keely. Especially after the way his and Keely's raising back and forth into each other after I'd committed myself to a pot had whipsawed me.

Keely smiled. A death's-head smile with his bleached teeth and tight-drawn skin. He put down his cards, face down and fanned close in front of him, put the two chips on top of them, and stood up.

Inside, I groaned. Was he really all that superstitious, or was he throwing more mud in my eyes to make me think he was holding nothing?

Keely walked around his chair, lifting his half-boots carefully over the small, heavy-handled sample case he seemed to have picked up since our landing.

He sat down, spat over his left shoulder. Then with a bony finger he pushed one card out of his fan, shoved the rest of them toward Hale.

"Four," he said, in his fat man's voice.

Hale and Morgan roared out laughing and I

wished that I could have joined them. Keely had bet into me like a man with a powerhouse and now he was asking for what was practically a new hand.

But he had his cards from Hale now and again he threw in his two chips. "I tap you."

I took my last two chips in my hand and if it's true that a drowning man sees his whole life flashing through his mind, then I might as well have been drowning.

Only I wasn't seeing my past, I was thinking of my future.

My future. Keely had my cameras in hock, the cameras I'd hoped to open up the star worlds with. Except that the star worlds didn't much seem to care if a balding, flabby ex-SpaceNav Photo Mate opened them up or not, so that I was already scraping before I even felt Keely's bony hand on my shoulder.

Now I was broke, even my Earthside passage-chit turned in to get the credits to sit in on this last game. If I lost, I'd be stranded on this transit-stop world called Poldrogi and my skin was crawling at the thought.

A transit-stop world is like any other place catering almost exclusively to people just passing through. There's lots of action and lots of credits flowing, but only between the natives and the transients. If you're a native, you've got your local bigwigs to look out for you. If you're a transient, you've got your money to do you the same service. But if you're just passing through and happen to go broke? Well, who can blame the locals if they take it out on you for the slights, the insults, the downright brutalities they've put up with from transients who are perhaps less sensitive but better brained than to get themselves stranded like me, Eli Pike.

I weighed the two credits in my hand. Two credits. Flitterfare from here to the launchport ... or one shot of Muscat. Two credits, my last.

I weighed them and looked at my cards. Looked at the inside straight, still empty in the middle and the eight I'd drawn. But it did match up with my outside card to give me a pair of them. A pair of eights against a four card draw.

I weighed my credits and looked at my cards and waited for my scalp wound to give me some kind of a hint. An itch, a tingle, anything, but I guess after all the ignoring I'd been giving it lately it was sulking.

Nothing.

I sighed and let my two credits fall into the pot. "I call," I said.

Keely grinned and laid down his cards face up. "I helped my hand a little on that draw," he said.

He didn't have to tell me. I could see his cards. Five of them, and all blue. He'd drawn four cards to fill out a flush.

Hale said it for me. "I see it, but I don't believe it." He dropped the deck he was still holding and glanced at me, looking uncomfortable. After all, Keely hadn't been exactly subtle about the way he was reaming me. "This kind of luck who can fight?"

I shoved back my chair and stood up. "That cleans me," I said and the knot in my stomach couldn't have been so hard after all. From the way I felt it shaking, it must be as soft as jelly. "See you around," I said and headed for Keely's door. All I wanted from his room right now was out.

"Pike! Hold on a minute." It was Keely's voice and it stopped me.

I turned. Morgan was rubbing the back of his head and Hale was on his feet, stretching. The game was obviously over. What did Keely want?

Keely waved me to a seat with one bony hand and when the others had gone, took the time to order up his lunch on the vid-com before he turned to me.

And I mean he took his time. I'd seen him study over the menu on the starship coming here, pulling out his lower lip, rubbing heads with the wine steward, even calling up the chef, so that I didn't fidget as much as I might otherwise have. The way Keely ate, his bones should have been lost in fat and not pushing hard through his skin.

I shook my head. "If I ate like that, I'd waddle," I said, and I was surprised to hear my voice come out unsteady. Maybe listening to Keely ordering all that food, and me not knowing where my next was coming from, had got me more unsettled than I thought.

Keely shrugged. "Each of us has his idiosyncrasy. Mine, I like to think, is at least endurable."

He leaned back in his chair and kept looking at me out of those bony-socketed, beady eyes of his until I put my hands on the arms of my chair and started to push myself up.

Keely held up both his thin hands. "Don't be so impatient," he said. "I think you'll find what I have to say to you well worth waiting to hear."

I hesitated, then dropped back again. If his purpose was to draw me out fine and snip off the knots before he let me in on what he had in mind, he was making it.

He lifted his half-booted foot and with it shoved the small sample case I'd been watching him step over each time he circled his chair for luck out into the clear. From the way it scraped the floor it was heavy. "I'd like you to do me a favor," he said.

I eyed the case. Black, shiny composition. About a foot high, and the same in the other two dimensions. Sturdy handle on top. It could pass for the case of one of my camera sync motors. But I'd bet no motor ever weighed what this box looked to.

"A favor? Like what?" I said, and I had all I could do to keep from reaching up and scratching the scar on the top of my head.

Keely was great on not answering questions. Instead he reached inside his tunic and came out with a short, compact-looking cylinder and stood it on the table right out in front of me.

Bright yellow. Everybody knew the bright yellow wrapping of the new double-eagle credit-coins. Fifty of them in that roll and I didn't need to see the bold black figures on the side to know that at twenty Earthbucks each I was staring at what was, for me, salvation.

Keely let me drool a long minute before he waved a hand at the roll. "Go ahead," he said. "Pick it up. See what it feels like."

I reached out, did as he said. The skinny devil with the fat man's voice knew the roll would have a nice heft to it, that if I picked it up, I might not be able to put it down.

But then Keely didn't know about my scar. I faked scratching it by rubbing it with the palm of my hand. I rubbed hard, but I had to give in.

I put the heavy roll of credits back on the table.

"No, thanks," I said and heaved myself out of Keely's chair and headed for his door.

"Fifty credits . . ." his fat voice followed me, ". . . and your cameras."

That stopped me. The cameras I'd lost to Keely in yesterday's game, mine again . . . and enough credits to get me back Earthside and, if I watched it, maybe a little left over.

So let my blasted scar itch. I turned back.

"You drive a hard bargain," I rasped. "Who do I kill?" and I wasn't really sure but that I wasn't half serious.

Keely laughed. "It's not that hard to take," he said and kicked at his black sample case. "Take this Earthside with you when you go. Give it back to me when you get there."

I stared at him, waiting for more.

"That's it," he said.

"What's in the box?" I said.

"You've got a license to transport communications equipment," he said, again not exactly answering me. "Put it among your cameras and nobody will look at it twice."

Keely was right about my having the license. Since the hard lesson of the last Peace Action, cameras, recorders, transmitters, anything larger than the personal limited range receivers most people carried had to be specially licensed. The licenses were hard to get, almost impossible, it was rumored, without a service record of some sort to prove one's dependability.

Keely knowing about my license was no surprise, all photographers had them, it might even be the reason he'd sought me out to begin with. But he could be wrong about his case not being noticed among my equipment, and I didn't need an itching scar to warn me about carrying pigs in pokes.

"Is it communications equipment?" I said.

He hesitated, then nodded. "Yes, of a sort."

I didn't believe him. I started for the door again. Being stranded on a transit-world might get me knifed in some dark alley, but it was only a maybe. If I lost my license to carry my cameras over Keely's box, then *that* would be a sure thing. What else did I know how to do to earn me eating credits?"

"Forget it," I said over my shoulder at Keely, half expecting him to try to stop me again.

He didn't. If he had, maybe I would have kept on going and gotten out of there. But he just snorted in a disgusted way, like he was mad at himself for being soft-headed enough to try to do someone a favor. "Suit yourself," he said, and folded his long bony fingers over the nonexistent paunch of his stomach.

Swearing at my scar, I turned back. I swept Keely's roll of credits into my tunic pocket, grabbed hold of his sample case to take it with me before I changed my mind again . . . and almost pulled my arm out of its socket.

The case did not budge.

With both hands I gripped the handle, squatting to lift with my legs so that its weight would not pop my back. This time I made it.

It weighed. I wouldn't care to estimate what it weighed, but it weighed, and, leaning over backward against the pull, I carried it from Keely's room, him opening the door for me and peering up and down the hall for some reason before he waved me on past him.

"You've got it now," he said and his voice wasn't

tight, or fat-sounding. Just cold, and the chill I felt I told myself came from the sweating his blasted case was making me do. "You've got it, don't lose it." And I heard him close and bolt his door behind me.

After the brightness of Keely's room the hall was dim, and when I came to the cross-corridor with my eye-bulging burden and saw the two squat figures step out of it toward me, I took them at first to be Hale and Morgan, and half wondered what they wanted.

But then I saw that the shorter of the two men had a kind of apelike shuffle to the way he walked, and I knew then it was not the two men I'd been playing poker with the past two days.

There was no preamble. The taller man just stepped close to me. "Give me that," he snapped and reached for Keely's case.

Maybe I still had some of the chill of Keely's voice chasing itself up and down my spine, or maybe it was just a reflex action. Unthinking, as reflex actions are.

"Give me that," he said, and I did. As he and his ape-walking buddy reached their ham hands for the handle of Keely's case I swung it.

I swung it like an athlete swings his hammer, and, Lord knows, I've photographed enough of them. But not as far. Inches, barely. Just far enough to give it a little arc when I let go of the handle.

It arced. Like the proverbial ton of bricks, it arced and landed on the bigger ape's foot.

I heard the crunch of bones with a completely human feeling of satisfaction.

Big Ape yelped. He grabbed at his leg with both

his hands and tried to yank his ruined foot out from under. He choked, gurgled, and went down.

He was out and a lucky thing for him it was. The human body can take just so much pain and then it cuts out. If his first yank hadn't knocked him out, the twisting of his trapped foot as he went down would have finished the job.

His ape-walking buddy goggled at the heap on the floor, then swung on me. "Why you ..." lifting both arms, hands outstretched, edges down like two huge meat cleavers rising up on either side of my head.

I'm no karate or judo or any such kind of expert. All the body combat training I ever had was the demonstration or two in SpaceNav boot camp that they marched me to and marched me away from while they were making up their minds whether to assign me to Cook and Baker's School or the Photo School on Pensa.

As it turned out, I went to neither. Someone fouled up cutting my orders and I went to an operational photo unit right out of boot.

But how much science does it take to come up with a knee just as the other guy is closing in on you?

Anyway, I did and I must have caught Ape-Walk where it hurts, because he turned green and grabbed himself. Which gave me the chance to come up under that craggy chin of his with my right hand in which, incidentally, I seemed to somehow be gripping the firm, hard roll of double-eagles I'd swept off Keely's table and dropped into my tunic pocket.

Ape-Walk went down, and I don't think it needed my boot at the side of his head to keep him there.

But I was worked up and not thinking, except maybe a fleeting thought about heaven help the expert in anything if he is stupid enough to go up against a worked-up tyro.

I got even more worked up when I saw what was in Keely's box that I might have gotten myself killed over.

The heavy falling must have sprung its lock because as I stepped around Ape-Walk and squatted down to lift with my legs and not my back, the lid flew up with my first tug and I was staring down into its small inside.

Empty! Completely empty, except for the two small fat coils wired together in the bottom that I recognized on sight even in the shaded hall light. I've used the gimmick often enough to anchor equipment under water or against a heavy wind.

Anti gravity coils, jury-rigged to reverse their polarity so that each one's field augmenting the other's made the case weigh like the backbreaker it did.

I reached down, ripped out the heavy jumper wire and the case was light in my hand as I stormed back to Keely's room.

"Keely," I shouted, pounding on his locked door, not much caring who heard the racket I was making. "Keely. Open up. It's Pike."

The door opened, suddenly, and I almost fell into the room.

I'd only been gone minutes, but it was long enough for Keely's food to have been brought up to him. At least I thought it was because he stood away from the door with a small kebab skewer in his fingers; on the end of it a tiny, brown, peanut-shaped carcass, and I didn't need the faintly sickening sweet smell nor the burning candle warmer on the table behind him, to know Keely was roasting for himself the contraband grubs of the Ra-Pak beetle.

And from the glaze in Keely's eyes I think I would have won a bet that he hadn't removed their venom sacs.

Ra-Pak grub venom. The fat, stinking grubs, roasted, were disgusting enough, but gourmets have been known to work up a fancy for eating many an oddball thing, earth and clay in ancient Spain, for example.

But the venom. That had an absinthe-like effect on the brain and moral fiber that made it a thing outlawed on any world that was not altogether depraved. Even here on Poldrogi I could think of no one who would traffic in the worms.

That meant that Keely must have brought his supply with him, and if he could get Ra-Pak grubs through customs, then what did he need me for to move an empty box?

I shoved the sample case up to his face with one hand, reached for his tunic front with the other. "Two apes," I started to say, but he'd stepped back and, if there had been any blood in his face to drain away, I think it would have done so when he saw me and the open case.

His mouth worked soundlessly and when the words finally came, it was more of themselves than of his volition. "Already? They caught up with you already?"

Then the glaze cleared from his eyes and he was his tight-drawn, snide self again. "Throw that thing away," he said, making a motion at the box I was holding under his thin nose. "I guess they're closer to me than I thought."

I dropped the case. Not on his foot, but on the floor. "They," I said. "Who're they? What did you suck me into? I've got a right to know."

Keely shrugged. "Rights," he said. "I made a play and I missed. You're fifty double-eagles ahead because of it. Keep them and forget it. Good-bye."

But those two apes out in the hall would come looking for me when they came to and I knew exactly nothing about what was going on. "Listen," I said to Keely, "I'm not going until. . . ."

"Move," Keely snapped, suddenly pointing at me the kebab skewer I'd surprised in his hand, the wormlike Ra-Pak grub still impaled on its point.

An eight inch skewer of steel, held daintily with a delicacy, no matter how repulsive, on its point is one thing. Settled firmly in the hand and pointing at your throat, it suddenly becomes a very convincing stiletto.

"Move," Keely said. "I won't tell you again."

I moved. Back and out. Again the door closed and was bolted behind me.

I did not go to see if the apes were still piled up on the hall floor, but instead went in the other direction. As far as the first cross-corridor.

I ducked into it, pulled my room key from my pocket, hung it by its ring on my finger in plain sight. If I heard someone coming I could start walking and obviously be a guest looking for his room. Meanwhile, I could stay where I was and keep an eye and an ear on Keely's room.

Sooner or later he would have to come out and if he didn't look to be staggering under any weight, then what I had to look for was still inside. Because it was beginning to dawn on me that Keely had selected me to carry his black box Earthside, not because he couldn't do it himself, secretly, but because my two hundred pounds of staggering flab couldn't be missed doing the same thing.

A decoy he'd meant me to be. A patsy. And now I was in it with Keely on one side of me and the apes, or whoever wanted something weighty from Keely, on the other. And now that I'd tangled with both sides, I stood a good chance of getting clobbered by either or both. Ignorant of what it was all about, but clobbered just the same.

The answer was in Keely's room, of that much I was sure. But to find it, I first had to get inside.

His lunch came, but from the other direction so I didn't need to use my "roving guest" dodge. The waiter rolled his cart into Keely's room and came out without it. I was too far away to hear Keely shoot home the bolt of his door behind him, but I was sure he had.

Having been witness to the almost obscene pleasure Keely took in his food, I expected a long wait, and he didn't disappoint me. My neck and shoulders were stiff with all the waiting and I was leaning them on the wall and shifting, and beginning to think that I had Keely figured wrong. That he was inside getting himself way out on grub venom and I could be here the rest of the day and all of the night. Just then he finally came out and went down the hall to the downflit, his skinny legs scissoring.

Unbolted on the inside, his door could now be unlocked from the hall by anyone who had a master to this tier. That meant the waiter who'd be coming back for his food cart.

I got myself ready for him by breaking open Keely's roll of double-eagles and distributing them loose in my tunic pockets. When he showed up and opened the door and went in, I was right on his heels, my hand in my side pocket.

"Keely?" I said to the room. "Keely? It's Pike. Where are you?"

The waiter turned on me, his eyes hostile. And then I saw the light come into them and knew he was hearing me jingling the double-eagles in my pocket with what I hoped would be taken for impatience. "Where is that guy?" I added for effect.

The waiter was very polite. "I'm afraid Mr. Keely isn't here," he said. "I think I passed him in the hall a few minutes ago."

You didn't pass him anywhere, friend, I said to myself. He was long gone before you showed up. But I dropped into Keely's chair behind his card table and looked at my wrist-chrono. "Then he'd better be getting back soon," I said. "I don't plan on waiting long."

The waiter started to say something, protest maybe about leaving me alone in Keely's room, but I stopped him. I stopped him by starting to take double-eagles from my various pockets where I'd stowed them and stacking them on the table in front of me, shoving aside what little Keely'd left of his meal to do so.

I looked up at the waiter. "Well," I said, "what are you waiting for?" I waved a hand at his cart and the empty dishes. "Clean up this mess and get out of here."

I held my breath and went on pulling credits from my pockets and stacking them and hoping that with all that hard loot piling up in front of me

I would not only look respectable to the waiter, but also as if I had a right to be where I was.

I must have. He mumbled, "Yessir," scooped his dishes onto his cart, and was gone. I didn't tip him because A, double-eagles was all I had and to flip him one of those for just letting me wait in Keely's room was too much and would make him suspect me of being a phony, and B, or maybe A again, a double-eagle was, after all, a double-eagle.

I barely waited for the waiter to close the door behind him before I was on my feet and rummaging in Keely's closet.

I didn't know what it was that I was looking for, but I was sure it would be small enough to fit into a one-foot-by-one-foot box and heavy. It might even look like the box itself.

Too heavy for the bottom of a hotel dresser drawer to support, and for the same reason not likely to be lifted onto a high closet shelf.

On the closet floor I looked, and on the closet floor I found it. A sturdy, metal-bound attache case, the only one of the bags stowed there with enough heft to it. I dragged it out of the closet darkness and into the light.

It was locked. I'd expected it to be. The locks, two, set deep in the plasti-leather. No prying them open.

Cut the case.

I looked around for something sharp, a skewer perhaps, but there were none in the drawers I hastily pulled out.

A skewer! Food! With Keely's rates and his appetites, his room had a wine cooler and when I opened it I saw I was in luck. A tall bottle was cooling.

I smashed it and took the broken neck to the side of the attache case. It cut but only through the plasti-leather. Underneath it, I hit the hardness of metal.

I sat back on my heels, puffing from my flab and my exertions, having it in mind to risk the reception committee maybe waiting for me in my room and to haul case and all there for a better go at the locks when I heard a fumbling at the door.

Escape!

I shoved the case across the floor to the window, flung open the sash, hefted the weighty case up onto the sill, lifted one leg over the edge after it.

Thirty-seven dizzy levels below was the nearest terrace and I balanced there, half in, half out, gripping the case that teetered on the sill in my sweaty palms.

The door burst open and Keely shot into the room. He tried to slam it shut, but the two men were too close behind him, thrusting him back as they smashed in.

Ape-Walk and a tall, blond man with a blaster. "Freeze," the blond one said, and Keely froze.

I couldn't believe it, but was Keely sobbing quietly? And then I saw his eyes were not on the man who menaced him, but riveted on the case teetering in my hands.

Sweaty hands that were having trouble gripping it because it kept trying to slip out of them.

Staring and saying over and over, "No. Oh, no."

The blond one with the blaster motioned at me with it. "Inside," he said, but I shook my head. "You want this case," I said. "I come back in and you take it and blast me. I stay here maybe you blast me anyway, but the case goes down with me if you do."

There was a long silence between us and then the blond one laughed. "Standoff. What do you want? A cut?"

"No, an explanation."

The pale eyes wavered, "An explanation?"

"Sure," I said and I was sweating. "Keely here set me up for some kind of patsy. All I want is to know what it was he suckered me into."

The two men were looking at me and at Keely. Out of the corner of my eye I saw a glint of light and the broken bottle neck I'd dropped by the closet door was somehow hurtling through the air and full at the tall man with the blaster.

In that instant I knew about Keely. About him and about a chip that fell of itself off the top of a pile, a skewer that settled itself in his hand, even about the attache case that seemed to want to free itself of my grasp on it. Keely could move things with his mind!

The hurtling bottle neck!

Without thinking, I yelled and the tall man dropped. The jagged glass missile missed his face and eyes by the scantest of margins, to go smashing against the wall.

Thinking or not, it turned out to be the smartest thing I'd done since I first saw Keely. But just now he looked to be flinging himself at me, bony arms outstretched, hands clawing.

I shoved myself into the room, pushing one way, the case flying the other. But Keely was past me and I thought out the window after the case.

He hung there straining. Straining until I heard the smashing sound from the terrace far below.

Then he fell back into the room, sliding down until he sat on the floor under the window and this time there was no mistaking the fact that the sounds coming from behind the hands covering his face were sobs.

The tall man was picking himself up from the floor, his face white. "I owe you for that," he said, and put away his blaster.

He looked at Keely sobbing on the floor and spat. "The pig," he said. "Serves him right. He did it to himself."

Later, back in my room, I was still shaking my head over what the blond man had told me of Keely and his strange talent ... and the even stranger use to which, driven by his compulsion to eat, yet smothering in inexorably swelling fat, Keely had put it.

Imperfectly, because his control was erratic, incomplete, taking along bits of nerve and other tissue, and cutting down on their bulk but not their weight by squeezing from them some of the space between their atoms, Keely had teleported to refri-jars he could carry in his double-locked case, the fat-bloated cells of his body.

And because a man does not grow obese by adding more cells to his body but by distending, with the by-products of his gluttony, those he already has, Keely could not bring himself to abandon these cells. And in the learning of this fact of Keely's mind, was born the blond man's plan.

What better to hold for a rich man's ransom than bits of his own body? And if caught? All they'd taken were a few refri-jars of oddly heavy human fat. A laboratory curiosity, but of no intrinsic value.

Certainly nothing worth the bother or the expense of prosecuting them for.

A direct and imaginative plan except, of course, it hadn't worked out. I shook my head. Well, the kidnappers, if you could call them such, were gone and so was Keely, spirited out the back way by the jittery hotel people, strapped in a psycho-cocoon and still sobbing.

I rubbed my hand over my balding head. I had no cameras and no illusions about getting them back from Keely when he got out of the psycho-home, if he ever did. But there was always a way and I could work on that. I had to.

I took my tunic from the back of the chair where I'd hung it. Fleetingly I wished that I had a better garment to put on than this out-of-date, travel-stained one but then, considering the way its pockets sagged with Keely's credits still distributed among them, it would do. It would do nicely.

I put it on, hearing the double-eagles make a lightly clicking and thoroughly comforting sound. In the doorway I stopped, taking, from habit, a last look around the room.

My scar tingled, but it definitely did not itch. I closed the door and went down the hall whistling, badly, an old SpaceNav chantey to which I'd forgotten the words and most of the tune.

Moire

> MOIRE: *An independent usually shimmering pattern generated when two geometrically regular patterns are superimposed.*

Six feet four, two hundred pounds, and able to swim about as well as a porous rock. All the same, I pressed myself down into the water from which the reeds sprang, listening.

Listening. Straining my ears in the heavy darkness until I thought the skin on the back of my neck would pop, knowing that the swelling and the lessening of the sounds those who were after me were making was not in their nearness or distance, but in me.

Warily, swearing inside at the way the strength in my hands would come and go, I started working at the base of the tall reed. Bending it, pulling it down slowly, ever so slowly, excruciatingly aware that in the night-vision glasses the men tracking me wore, a movement, unless it was heartbreakingly slow, would show with a sudden yellow flaring against the dull red of the overall background stillness.

"Pike," someone shouted, his voice coming at a low point in my hearing, but I knew my own name well enough. "Pike. Come out. Give yourself up. Don't make us come in after you."

I kept working on the reed, pulling it down slowly, fearful it would slip through my hands, the motion of its snapping erect betraying my location as brightly as if I'd sent up a rocket flare.

At last I had it flat and hidden, close to my body. And now I twisted it, fighting my hands and their unsure grip that was making of its toughness so formidable an opponent; fighting to keep my lungs from gasping out their air and making the high grasses around me tremble. Make them tremble and have the motion betray me to my pursuers.

Slowly, slowly, but hurry, before they can bring up their heat detectors and use your own body's warmth for a beacon to home in on.

The reed was free in my hands. I strangled my gasp of relief and, waiting until I could feel it firm in my grip, broke off its tip. Then, raising one end to my mouth, I blew into it.

I blew, feeling my cheeks puff out and straining until the pinpoints of light danced red and yellow in my eyeballs and the strength of my lungs ebbed away.

Nothing. The reed was plugged. *Membranes crossing its diameter.*

Sweating, I groped in the darkness for another reed. Thin but sturdy.

I found one, pulled it down and worked it free as carefully as I'd done the first even though now I could hear, dimly, and then more clearly, and dimly again as my hearing phased in and out, the unmistakable beat of approaching hover-craft.

Using the thinner reed as a reamer, I poked into the larger one, first from one end and then from the other. Again I blew into it. And this time my breath moved unobstructed. The inner passage of the long reed was clear.

Carrying my new-made tube, and stopping only when it threatened to slip from my fingers, I groped in the darkness for deeper water. Oddly enough, even though no one, not even the SpaceNav Specialists back in my Service days, in Boot and elsewhere, had been able to teach me to swim, I had no particular fear of deep water. And even if I had, the hover-craft racket now clear in the night behind me, would have given me reason enough to press on anyway.

From the sound of things, it was plain to me that I'd had just about as much time as I was going to get to find out how deep the weed-choked semi-swamps that were the lakes of Poldrogi could get.

I found a clump of weeds that felt thicker than the rest, and, blowing through my reed to clear it, put one end among them so that it might better escape the notice of my pursuers. The other end I put in my mouth and, pinching my nose between my fingers as best their phasing would let me, I settled myself down, the black water closing over my head, plugging my ears with its characteristic roar, until I sat on the silted and treacherous-feeling bottom.

They would not come after me, I hoped, once they'd lost me in their night-glasses, until there was enough light to see me by. I was lucky, I suppose, not to be on Linden or Ogden or any of the more fashionable planets where sceni-lights came on automatically as a human approached. But Poldrogi was, after all, only a transit-world, a place to wait out starship connections and, aside from the anti-crime lights in the city itself, its Council of Peers would not waste power on lighting up the countryside.

All I could do for now was wait, the hover-craft, their heat detectors dangling beneath them, criss-crossing over my head. Wait in the pulsing water, and hope that my breath, traveling the length of the reed I'd selected, would emerge in a wisp cool enough to escape detection.

Wait, ignoring the things that bumped and slithered against me in the blackness, wait and think and wonder what there was about me that got me into messes like this anyway. I already knew *how* I got into them.

I got into them by not paying the scar on the top of my head the attention I should have, by this time, learned it deserved. The medic who'd patched me up during the Second Peace Action had done a better than good job and you could barely see its thin line and then only when the light shone right on my balding head.

But I knew the scar was there. I knew it every time it itched when I was about to do something more stupid than usual. Something that, if I was lucky, would only get me a few lumps to keep it company on my head.

But that girl.

I was standing in my hotel corridor, waiting for the downflit and running over in my mind what I might find to eat, when she put her hand on my arm.

My eyes, like any photographer's, automatically checked the bones of her wrist under its real-fur bangle, knowing from their structure that the ankles in those pipestem boots the women were wearing this season would be well worth the looking at.

"Mi-ister Pike? Mister Eli Pike?"

She spoke hesitantly, her voice matching her bones, speaking Intergalactic English with an accent I couldn't quite place, yet somehow I sensed in it a land lying open and prostrate under the heat of a punishing sun.

This kid was no corridor-walker, that was for sure. I rubbed my head. So why, all of a sudden, was my scar itching?

"Yes," I said. "I'm Pike."

"Good," she said and smiled. "Could we go somewhere . . . and talk?"

This is where I should have cut out, the way my scar started acting up. But I just pressed it hard with my palm, faking the scratching. Don't be silly, I said to myself, and maybe to my scar. If this is what trouble looks like, then where do I line up for my share.

But aloud I said, "I'm just on my way for something to eat. Would you join me, Miss. . . ?"

As they used to say in the old, old books, she dimpled at me. "Mrs.," she said. "Mrs. Corse." And I knew right then that in spite of the way she looked and sounded, this was going to be business.

It was. An assignment, and one so simple that I wondered why she felt she needed a pro.

Anton Corse. A man with a big bankroll and a bigger heart. I had to take her word for that, although being his wife she should certainly know. But I suppose that a man didn't go to the trouble of learning magic just so that he could go from planet to planet, from health home to health home, putting on shows for the shut-ins without there being something in his heart aside from the blood it was pumping.

They were on Poldrogi now, Anton and she, and tonight he planned an after-supper show for the children at the Wayfarer's Home. Could I ... would I photograph his performance so that she, Soledad, could add the pictures to her scrapbook?

"Tri-D?" I asked.

"No," Soledad said. Simple, uni-angle shots were all she wanted, and I was all the more puzzled. My last caper with a telepath named Keely had cost me my cameras and just about everything else I owned, but even aside from that, the way she was pulling credits out of her shoulder purse made it hard for me to say no. I was sure I could find a camera, a small correspondent's unit perhaps, that would do the job.

I nodded. "It's a deal," I said, hoping she wouldn't think I was some kind of a nut the way I was rubbing my palm on my itching scar.

A camera was not hard to find. Poldrogi, like any world where people were apt to run out of ready credits, had its share of Medici-marts, so called because their centuries-old symbol of three golden balls was supposed to have been taken from that family's escutcheon.

I selected a correspondent-type camera, larger than most carried, but I liked an insta-back that let me see what I'd caught before I permanentized my image. I tested its controls a few times, checked the field and alignment of the fill-in unit, thought of leaving the recharging of its image chamber until later and then decided to have it done now. I might not need it, but I liked working with a fully-charged chamber whenever I could.

It was still light when I got to the Wayfarer's Home, but they had their lawn lights on full and the place was hip deep in kids, all yelling and shouting. In the middle of all the furor a good-sized platform was floating about a yard and a half off the ground and when I saw that I nodded my approval.

Long ago, when I was only a little bigger than these children crowding all around me, magic had been a pretty serious interest with me, and I liked to see the work of a man who knew what he was about. There is nothing like seeing space under a performer's stage to put a thing like trapdoors or hidden assistants out of an audience's minds.

On the platform was a covered shape, man-high and vaguely familiar, although I couldn't at the moment place what it reminded me of.

I felt a hand placed lightly on my arm and looked down to see Soledad smiling up at me. She said something, but I couldn't make out what it was in all that din. I held up a hand, then I picked up a small pebble and tossed it under the floating platform.

To hold up a stage with ordinary hover units was out of the question, of course, the way their blast churned up the dust and debris and everything else in its path. But you could use antigrav units or put your platform on a solid base and then mask it with the crisscrossing rays of dozens of tiny refraction units. Either way ate power and cost the proverbial satchelful.

The path of the pebble I'd thrown glowed faintly blue for a moment and I knew Corse was using antigrav units and that there really was no place under his stage to conceal an assistant.

"You are a man of no small curiosity," Soledad laughed when we were free of the midget crowd and I could hear her. Nosy would have been a better word for her to use, I thought, but I wasn't about to mention it to her. I smiled and let her lead me by the arm into the dome-shaped main building.

Anton Corse was a small man, compactly built, the way they're breeding them on the rim planets these days where, I suppose, the efficient use of feed and living space is, after all, of prime importance. But Corse looked a bit old for that to have been the case with him although, after seeing Soledad, maybe I'd just expected him to be a much younger man.

He had thick white hair built high on his head and a thin white mustache to go with it. He wore the standard electric-blue evening tights with a short silver jacket, both of them cut in a way that made you think the words "superbly tailored" were invented just so you could say what he looked like.

With him were three or four other men, in ordinary yellow and blue tunics, compactly built like himself, but all young, tough looking.

Philanthropist Corse might be, and here to give a few moments of pleasure to some unfortunate children, but I knew a phalanx of bodyguards when I saw one and, for that matter, so did my scar. But with Soledad on my right arm and my camera in my left hand, there wasn't much I could do but let it itch.

Soledad did not introduce us, nor, for that matter, did Corse even so much as nod in her direction when we came into the main hall, although if I'd been in his place I think I'd have a done a bit more than nod if a wife of mine came in anywhere hanging on anybody's arm the way Soledad was on mine. Although I suppose I should have been happy that Corse didn't seem to mind because, now that I was well inside the hall I saw that there were other young men scattered around, all conservatively dressed in yellow and blue until the ordinary business tunics began to look to me like some kind of unobtrusive uniform.

But Soledad had slid open the door to what looked like a small anteroom and was taking the camera from my hand. I didn't want to let it go, but I supposed that with all of the bully boys that seemed to be thronging the place, it was safe enough on the small table beside Soledad's shoulder purse.

"A small drink," she said, "while we wait." And sure enough, on the low table in front of a narrow divan were glasses and a tall bottle, oddly shaped, that made my mouth water just to look at it.

But I never got to find out if what was in it tasted like its outside looked. Soledad had just about got me settled on the divan when the door she'd closed behind her slid open and one of the bully boys stuck in his head.

He spoke with the same strange accent as Soledad, but heavier by far. His message was plain enough. The master wanted me on stage and ready when he made his entrance and that was right now.

I sighed and followed the bully boy, noticing half-absently when I picked up my camera that it felt vaguely different in my hand, but then, it was a strange camera and after carrying it for as long as I had before Soledad took it from me, I suppose I expected it to feel warmer than it did.

On the floating platform the man-high shape was now uncovered and I saw why it had looked familiar to me. I should have known it instantly, covered or uncovered, because my previous seeing of it had cost me more Earthbucks than I could think of without breaking out in a sweat.

From a small round base a foot or so high and just big enough around for a man to stand his feet on, sprouted four thin rods that looked to be made of pitted and rusted iron. Flaring upward and outward they could be adjusted, I knew, for height.

I looked around for its mate. It had to be close by somewhere, because the blasted money-sucking thing couldn't be made to work over any appreciable distance. Sure enough, just behind the stage, less than a dozen feet away, stood a decorated kiosk, a screened walk leading from it back to the side of the domed main building.

Anton Corse, Magician, was going to make his entrance in a puff of smoke and a burst of flame, most likely, right smack in the middle of a floating and otherwise open stage. And he was going to use August Rook's matter transmitter to do it.

August Rook and his matter transmitter. I remembered it all right. I and a whole planetful of saps who bought up the stock of the company his brother-in-law, Barney, formed to finance August's work, as fast as he could get the shares out to us. We were all going to be fantastically rich.

Think of it, Barney kept telling us. No more space craft and their long warp-journeys, no more Earth craft or even visi-phones, for that matter. Why waste the effort of a call to someone when you could step into your Rook Transmitter and be there beside him instantly to talk all you wanted.

The shipping industry was ruined, of course, and so was almost any means of moving, or talking, of communicating, that you could think of. Oh, it was going to have a dramatic and pregnant effect on life, was August's device. As soon as he could get the bugs out, that is.

Rook had developed an electronic pencil ray that he claimed could scan and strip away whatever he placed in its field, molecule by molecule; convert this matter to energy that could be transmitted to a matching unit at a distance and there be converted back again, layer by layer, molecule by molecule, until the original object was recreated.

But lay an anesthetized mouse on its side and it stacks up to a lot of layers of molecules. To scan them one by one took time, lots of time.

It also took power. Lots of power and the lights in his whole sector went to candle dimness when Rook turned on his device to demonstrate it to still another batch of prospective backers. If some curmudgeon brought this up, the great man would shrug his meaty shoulders and ask us for more of our Earthbucks to lay out for heavier and heavier power lines and more equipment. After all, once he'd demonstrated the workability of the basic principle in his lab, wasn't it just a question of engineering from there on in?

Maybe it was and maybe it wasn't. Anyway, all engineering seemed able to come up with was, by using multiple scanners all synchronized to a split micro-wavelength, to cut down the scanning and reconstituting time to a reasonable few seconds.

And the objects August could handle did grew larger, too.

But his transmitter still drained power. Oh, how it drained power. And its range? Rook's unit seemed to work on a law of its own that had the inverse square decrease look almost like an actual buildup by comparison. A small boy with a front tooth missing could throw a spitball farther than Rook could transmit it.

Where Rook was now I didn't know. But here, Anton Corse was using his transmitter to amuse children. Well, the distance between the transmitter hidden in the kiosk and the one onstage in front of me was short enough so that he could do it, if he didn't mind the cost. And from what I'd seen of Soledad's husband, he looked as though he didn't need to.

On Poldrogi the night, like that of Earthside Africa, falls fast, and beyond the flood-lighted lawn it was already darkening when, from the upright transmitter rods, I heard a low hum and knew that the unit and its hidden mate were being readied for Corse to make his magical appearance.

From long habit, I made a last minute check of my camera and like a craftsman who can pick up a tool from a benchful of others looking exactly like it and know it at once to be his own; as an Army sergeant in ancient British India could save the life of a visiting dignitary by detecting, as it passed through his hands in its automatic weapon belt, a dangerously damaged bullet; so I felt in my camera a strangeness as I lifted it to my face.

I lifted it, half wondering how, on an open lawn, there could be a draft to bring a sense of coolness to my cheek and eye.

On the rim of my vision I saw a motion and looked up to see Soledad waving frantically at me from the crowd. I shook my head and made signs to let her know I was just checking my distance and angle settings.

But still the camera felt strange in my hands and without thinking about it, I pointed it downward and squeezed its release.

I pointed it down from long habit to keep the momentary flash of its fill-in lights low and out of the gathered children's eyes.

I squeezed the release and saw the hole appear in the platform at my feet.

Startled, I jumped backward and heard, whirring through the space I'd just vacated, a sound I hadn't heard since the Second Peace Action. I heard the thin, nasty growl of a sniper's weapon and my body, remembering its combat-learned reflexes, started to drop me flat to the floor of the suddenly tilting and pitching stage.

As I went down, I could see that the hole at my feet was no longer a simple perforation, but a snaking, living gash. In a flash of understanding, as brilliant as only hindsight can be, I knew the reason for the feeling of coolness on my cheek.

In that same flash I knew a lot of things.

I knew, for example, where Soledad and her accent came from. From the Guadal cluster of worlds under whose merciless double sun blood runs hot and honor high.

I knew that only while my camera had rested on the small hall table beside Soledad's shoulder purse could someone have had the chance to remove the heart unit from my fill-in light and snap in its place a mini-laser. A mini-laser whose tight beam would pierce anything in its rosy path.

And I marveled at his or their audacity to use so hoary a dodge as to conceal a weapon in a camera; a dodge that, except for my sensing a strangeness in the feel of my camera, might have worked, perhaps because of its very obviousness.

Whoever had done this job had teamed the laser with a refri-unit. And I didn't need to be a cryogenics expert to know that under the extremely low temperature, a current flow set up in certain metals, once started, would not stop ... and the laser in my hand was still slashing.

Slashing and, from the platform's pitching and rolling, it must be playing havoc with the antigrav units that held it floating.

I fought to keep the laser pointed down and away from the now roiling, screaming mass of children around me. Swearing at the animals who, to kill a man, would choose a weapon that, like a hose that could not be turned off, would spray its death at the youngsters gathered around him.

I was flat on the pitching and rolling platform now. Over and around me was the obscene-sounding blat of police stun guns. Rook's transmitter, teetering, falling toward me, its bee-hum plain now even through the shouting and the screaming.

The pitching ... the blatting ... the transmitter keeling over ... toward me. Lord, let its insulation not be damaged ... not be grounded.

Dizziness hit me. A retching, tearing dizziness of unbearable seconds' duration and, the screaming and the uproar still in my ears, I was somehow falling to strike in a heap on solid ground.

I clung to it, digging into the earth with clawed

fingers, shaken still by the buffeting and the racking dizziness.

And then I knew where I was. Falling, Rook's transmitter had enveloped me in its field and I had just been dropped from its mate in the concealing shelter of the kiosk behind the stage.

I scrambled to my feet in the relative darkness ... at least I tried to, but my feet and my arms and my body ... everything about me felt at once oddly weak and strong and weak again in a strangely surging manner.

I tried again and this time I made it. I ran.

I ran toward the house, crouching and hidden by the screens that had been set up to mask the path of Anton Corse's entry onstage.

I ran on my odd-feeling feet, noticing now that the sounds behind me seemed to rise and fall, rise and fall. I ran intent as much upon escaping, as upon getting to Anton Corse to warn him from what quarter had come the aborted attempt upon his life.

The sniper's blast had told me that, once I'd squeezed my camera release and started the laser circuit, it wasn't intended that I be around to protest that I hadn't known it was there. Even my setting it off unexpectedly hadn't caught the sniper much off guard. Only my jumping back at the sight of the hole had saved me.

I ran, and only as I was about to crash into the building did I suddenly remember the bully boys and the fact that, for all they knew, it was I who'd intended to blast Corse and had betrayed myself only by some freak accident.

Then I remembered that it had to be one of them who'd switched the laser in the first place, in which case he ... or they ... had to blast me on sight to keep me quiet.

I was at the end of the concealing screens. Like all health homes, this one had no plantings close against its base. All its outside lights were on now, lights designed to show up a fleeing patient, and there were no shadows to dart in and out of.

Perhaps if I did not run, but moved purposefully, pretended to be one of the searchers looking for myself? After all, how many of them could recognize a Rook Transmitter for what it was and not take it to be merely a magician's stage dressing?

I'd vanished from the stage. They would be looking for me to be somewhere around it, not here by the building.

I had no choice but to brazen it out. It was that or take to my heels in headlong flight.

I gathered my oddly ebbing and flowing, ebbing and flowing strength, took a deep, wavering breath ... and stepped out into the blazing ground lights.

I stepped out and even before I heard the shout I knew I'd made a mistake.

They might not have known who I was ... or what I was. But to them I looked unmistakably strange.

To them and to myself.

In the dimness of the sheltering screens I had felt it, but I hadn't seen it. In the blazing lights it was dizzyingly, heart-stoppingly plain.

Over my body, my tunic, my boots ... my arms and hands when I stretched them out in front of my unbelieving eyes ... coursed, like rippling water, waves of visibility and ... nothingness.

Not true nothingness, because I could not see through the blurred and empty spaces, but a grayness, a lack of being that matched a weakness to its rippling passage. I looked, to myself at least, like a badly out of phase TriV holo projection.

I ran. Swearing at Rook and his miserable invention. Swearing at would-be assassins. Swearing most of all at myself for not heeding the warning of my scar when I first felt Soledad's light touch upon my arm.

I ran, dodging, falling, changing my direction, hearing the sounds of pursuit grow and diminish and never knowing if they were really falling behind or if it was just my own flawed hearing playing me false. I ran, evading yet never losing my pursuers until I stumbled, in the darkness, into the black and weed-choked waters of a Poldrogi lake.

I sat now on its bottom, breathing through a reed, waiting for those who were after me to tire of their search. Tire, though not enough to abandon it. They would never do that. For all they knew I was the beast who had callously placed the lives of their children in terrible danger, and they were relentless in their determination to get me.

But tire enough to set up a guard and wait for daylight. Tire enough to give me a slim chance to get away.

To get away and search out Anton Corse, first at the Home where I'd seen him last; elsewhere if he was already gone. In Corse, I felt, was my only chance to get off the hook his wife had hung me on. He might blast first and listen afterward, but then again he might not. From what I'd seen of him, he was no dreamy-headed bridegroom. The old husband, roving-eyed young wife bit might even have already occurred to him in relation to himself, else why hadn't he so much as glanced at Soledad when she'd come into the health home hall hanging on my arm.

Around me the water had stopped churning and cautiously, very cautiously, I raised my head clear of it enough to listen.

The hover-craft, their heat detectors dangling, sounded as though they were now searching the area directly across the lake.

Fine. That was exactly what I probably would have done had I been able to swim. Strike out across the lake in the dark and hope to escape up the opposite bank.

But I couldn't swim so, breathing though my reed, walking where the water was deep enough, slithering on my hands and stomach where it wasn't, I made my way along the same bank of the lake that held my pursuers, hoping they would feel that I would not be so stupid as to do just that.

It was slow going and treacherous, but I was sure my life depended on it, and with that incentive in mind, I held to it, phasing weakness and all.

I was clear of the voices now, surprised, a little, to have heard among them those of children, and so I crawled and hid, knowing that I had searching for me not a posse but a mob.

I crawled, expecting every moment to hear a scream of discovery, to feel the blast of a stun gun. Even when I saw again, still brightly lighted, the dome of the health home, I did not feel a sense of accomplishment.

It looked deserted, but when I crawled closer, I saw on the front lawn, the blazing white hair and stocky figure of Anton Corse; behind him a bully boy, standing easy, a stubby ray-carbine cradled in his arms.

Corse was standing, head erect, hands clasped behind his back, seemingly oblivious to the man behind him, on the edge of the now-grounded platform of his stage. His transmitter still lay toppled and I knew that it could not be touched until the tremendous potential it always built up in use could be discharged into the ground or allowed to dissipate. My camera, if it was there at all, I could not see.

But there was something in the rigid stance of Corse's silver jacketed, compact body that made the hackles on my neck start to rise.

I crawled, the simple act made difficult by my phasing strength, heading for the far side of the building, hoping that everyone really had joined the mob looking for me and that the building was as deserted as it looked.

I crawled, faster now with the building between me and the men on the stage. Through the building I went and along the still-screened way until at last I crouched, sweat-drenched and shaking from my ordeal, in the kiosk and next to the second of the paired transmitters, the wow-ing quality of its hum warning me that, discharging, it was potentially more dangerous than with the power full on.

Now to talk to Corse I had but to get the carbine from his bully boy before he could blast me with it.

I had neither the time nor the inclination for subtleties and I knew I had better act before what little good sense I had got the better of me. I bunched myself together and leaped.

Out of the kiosk I leapt and at the back of the

bully boy. He was young, he was tough, he might have been fast, but he was small and he was relaxed. I was six four, I weighed two hundred, and I was desperate. I bowled him over as he turned, my hands on his carbine, keeping it off me. I rolled back, twisting it from him, hoping my phasing grip would not fail me, slamming the butt up under his chin.

And then I was on my feet, the weapon in my hands, the bully boy limp at my feet.

Corse had turned to face me and I saw in his eyes naked terror ... or was it arrogance?

I didn't stop to ponder. The bully boy was out, but I didn't know for how long and I didn't want to use the ray-carbine in my hands. I had to talk fast.

"Your wife ..." I started to say to Corse, but he stopped me with his voice.

"I have no wife," he said and I was stunned.

Stunned, and in the split moment that I stood, figuratively open-mouthed, Corse leapt. Moving lightning fast, as only a small man can, he leapt toward the Rook Transmitter.

"No!" I shouted, but I was too late. He vanished. In a blinding, searing, ozone-smelling flash of raw current, the toppled transmitter grounded through Corse, gave off its built-up charge in one snarling burst, and with that burst went the energy pattern that had been Anton Corse.

Back Earthside, compliments of a jittery Poldrogi Council of Peers who would rather not have it bruited about that someone had selected their planet to try a bit of skulduggery on, particularly since it hadn't come off. I sat on a gantry in August

Rook's lab. It was his transmitter, he was the one I trusted to check me out for its aftereffects.

"What happened to me?" I said to him, waving away a glass of what looked like orange juice but which I knew wasn't that his brother-in-law, Barney, was trying to hand me.

August is tall, like myself, but portly. Barney is thinner, shorter.

August tossed my tunic at me. "Put your clothes back on," he said, "You're bald, not blonde."

I held my tunic up. It wasn't phasing. Neither were my hands and it felt good to hold something and not expect it to slip through your fingers.

"So she really was his wife," Barney said in his reedy voice.

"Maybe he said she wasn't to snap me off guard." I shrugged. "Way I look at it, it would have been better for him if it hadn't. August, what happened to me?"

"It could be because she'd failed him he was putting her out of his mind," August said.

"He was a power hungry nut," I said. "Some of his own people were onto him and I guess he figured he could get rid of them if he had something heinous to hang on them. An attempted assassination, particularly a messy one with maybe lots of innocent kids getting chewed up, looked like a classic way to him and he took it."

Barney shook his head. "He took a big chance. You might have nailed him before his sniper nailed you."

I wished Barney would shut up about Corse and let August tell me what had happened to me, but I answered him. "Not likely. He knew what to expect and when, I didn't."

I looked at August. "You didn't warn him about your transmitter?"

"Of course I did," he protested. "But who knows what he was thinking when he jumped. Maybe all that was in his mind was to escape and he forgot for the moment. Maybe when he saw you still alive, standing over his bully boy with a weapon in your hands, it hit him all at once how badly he'd failed and what his enemies would do to him now."

He shrugged his fat shoulders. "You said he was power hungry. He wouldn't be the first such to take that way out."

Barney was handing me his orange juice again. "Try it," he urged. "It's something new."

I wished he'd stop bugging me, it was making my scar itch. "Me," I said to August. "What happened to me?"

August laughed. "You got moired."

"I got what?"

"Moired. You know I have a scanner in each of the uprights of my transmitter."

I didn't, exactly, but I did know he was always talking about how precise the alignment of the various components of his device had to be in relation to each other. I nodded.

"Well," August was saying, "with all that tumbling and pitching and falling over, the units got knocked a little out of whack, their beams a little out of alignment, slightly overlapping each other."

He laughed. "You transmitted in one piece, but you fell out of the receiving end looking like a piece of watered silk."

"Very funny," I said. I didn't appreciate his humor.

"You don't know how lucky you are," Barney cut

in. "A shade more misalignment and the beams might have missed bits of you entirely. You'd have been transmitted in slices, the missed parts staying behind in the one transmitter, parts of you going over to the other. Like sliced ham."

"Ham," August said.

I shivered. What a way to go. Talk about topping the sawing-a-woman-in-half bit. I wished Barney would shut up ... and stop trying to shove that blasted glass of orange glop into my hand.

"Ham," August said. "Candied yams, maybe."

I wouldn't say I saw him lick his chops, but I wouldn't say I didn't. August didn't get to the size he is just thinking about food.

"There's a place down on the nineteenth level ... you wouldn't believe what they can do with the hind end of a pig. Finish dressing, I'll take you."

I was just about through with my clothes. Barney was shoving his glass in my hand. "Your juice. Don't forget your juice."

I sighed. There seemed to be no way to get rid of him but one. Besides, he was definitely making my scar itch. I took his concoction from his hand and gulped it down, gave Barney back his glass. I looked pointedly at him and said to August, "Let's go. For *your* kind of food I'm always ready."

I stood up, stamped my feet to settle my half-boots on them. "Moired," I said to August. "What do you mean, like a piece of watered silk?"

"Well," he said. "You've seen it on your tri-v when some clown who ought to know better wears a tunic with a small pattern to it. The beam picks it up and when it comes back for its between the lines fill-in run the patterns sort of overlap and you get that shimmering rainbow effect. What happened to you was...."

Sort of, I said to myself, that is what I call putting it in precise scientific language. But I wasn't about to interrupt August. Sort of.

Aloud I said, "Yes. Like a piece of watered silk ... moired."

DAW
Tales of the Rim-Worlds™

Frank A. Javor

☐ **THE RIM-WORLD™ LEGACY *AND BEYOND***
(UE2505—$4.50)
Long unavailable, here once again is the classic, award-winning novel that introduced Eli Pike to the annals of SF. Ex-SpaceNav photographer, now a free-lancer low on credits, Pike was always ready for a new assignment if the price was right. But what should have been an easy job, suddenly turned into a free-for-all with laser beams flying that sent Pike fleeing for his life from a host of people who thought he had the secret to an invention which could give its user unlimited power. As an added bonus, the volume includes two Eli Pike short stories.

☐ **SCOR-STING** (UE2421—$3.95)
His name is Pike, and he is a free-lance holojournalist in an age when media communication is strictly controlled. Called upon for aid by comrades from his military past, Pike finds himself on a planet hostile to human life, where the most important discovery to the future of the human race *may* lie hidden among storm-swept desert dunes. Is it real—or is it just a scam? Either way, it could be worth Pike's life to find out. . . .

☐ **THE ICE BEAST** (UE2443—$3.95)
Thul—an iceball of a world that Eli Pike had never planned to return to. But a free-lance holo journalist can't pass up a possible scoop, especially if he's short of funds—not even a crazy tale of the ultimate racing beast, being bred and trained in the wilds of Thul. But Pike's search takes a dangerous new turn when he stumbles upon a strange tribe determined to stay hidden from the rest of the galaxy at any cost.

PENGUIN USA
P.O. Box 999, Bergenfield, New Jersey 07621

Please send me the DAW BOOKS I have checked above. I am enclosing $_____
(check or money order—no currency or C.O.D.'s). Please include the list price plus $1.00 per order to cover handling costs. Prices and numbers are subject to change without notice. (Prices slightly higher in Canada.)

Name_____
Address_____
City _____ State _____ Zip _____
Please allow 4-6 weeks for delivery.

DAW
Epic Tales of Other Worlds

ELUKI BES SHAHAR

☐ HELLFLOWER (UE2475—$3.99)

Butterfly St. Cyr had a well-deserved reputation as an honest and dependable smuggler. But when she and her partner, a highly illegal artificial intelligence, rescued Tiggy, the son and heir to one of the most powerful of the hellflower mercenary leaders, it looked like they'd finally taken more than they could handle. For his father's enemies had sworn to see that Tiggy and Butterfly never reached his home alive....

DORIS EGAN

☐ THE GATE OF IVORY (UE2328—$3.95)

Cut off from her companions and her ship, attacked and robbed, anthropology student Theodora of Pyrene finds what began as a pleasure trip becoming a terrifying odyssey on the planet Ivory, where magic works. For all her studies and training are useless, and she is forced to turn to fortune-telling to survive. To her amazement, she discovers that she is actually gifted with magical skill—a skill, however, that will plunge her into deadly peril.

JOHN STEAKLEY

☐ ARMOR (UE2368—$4.50)

Impervious body armor had been devised for the commando forces who were to be dropped onto the poisonous surface of A-9, the home world of mankind's most implacable enemy. But what of the man inside the armor? This tale of cosmic combat will stand against the best of Gordon Dickson or Poul Anderson.

PENGUIN USA
P.O. Box 999, Bergenfield, New Jersey 07621

Please send me the DAW BOOKS I have checked above. I am enclosing $_____ (check or money order—no currency or C.O.D.'s). Please include the list price plus $1.00 per order to cover handling costs. Prices and numbers are subject to change without notice. (Prices slightly higher in Canada.)

Name_____

Address_____

City _____ State _____ Zip _____

Please allow 4-6 weeks for delivery.

DAW

NEW DIMENSIONS IN SCIENCE FICTION

Kris Jensen

☐ **FREEMASTER (Book 1)** (UE2404—$3.95)
The Terran Union had sent Sarah Anders to Ardel to establish a trade agreement for materials vital to offworlders, but of little value to the low-tech Ardellans. But other, more ruthless humans were about to stake their claim with the aid of forbidden technology and threats of destruction. The Ardellans had defenses of their own, based on powers of the mind, and only a human such as Sarah could begin to understand them. For she, too, had mind talents locked within her—and the Free-Masters of Ardel just might provide the key to releasing them.

☐ **MENTOR (Book 2)** (UE2464—$4.50)
Jeryl, Mentor of Clan Alu, sought to save the Ardellan Clans which, decimated by plague, were slowly fading away. But even as Jeryl set out on his quest, other Clans sought a different solution to their troubles, ready to call upon long-forbidden powers to drive the hated Terrans off Ardel.

Cheryl J. Franklin

☐ **FIRE CROSSING** (UE2468—$4.99)
Three immortal wizards had reversed the flow of time to set the Taormin matrix in its proper place, reopening a long-sealed time-space portal to the science-ruled universe of Network. Could one young wizard with a reputation for taking too many risks evade the traps of a computer-controlled society, or would he and his entire world fall prey to forces which even magic could not defeat?

PENGUIN USA
P.O. Box 999, Bergenfield, New Jersey 07621

Please send me the DAW BOOKS I have checked above. I am enclosing $_____ (check or money order—no currency or C.O.D.'s). Please include the list price plus $1.00 per order to cover handling costs. Prices and numbers are subject to change without notice. (Prices slightly higher in Canada.)

Name _____

Address _____

City _____ State _____ Zip _____

Please allow 4-6 weeks for delivery.